Caffeinated Murder
By Lynne Waite Chapman

ISBN: 978-1-952661-01-3

Chapter One

I don't imagine Officer Farlow expected the call that came into the Evelynton Police Department, that morning. The frantic report of a dead body found in a dumpster.

Small Midwest towns, like Evelynton, Indiana get lulled into a false sense of security. Going years without serious crime, they grow proud of their relative peace and tranquility. Our mayor had even boasted this was the perfect place to raise a family. Residents felt free to take long walks after dark. Few would lock their doors, on the off chance a neighbor might want to drop off a pie, or borrow a plunger.

In the interest of full disclosure, the last few years in this little town hadn't been quite so serene. In the first three years after I'd moved back to my hometown, there had been three suspicious deaths. One each year. The last had occurred almost exactly a year ago, so this gruesome discovery seemed to be right on schedule.

I'm afraid our police force had begun to believe the

job consisted of little more than traffic tickets and noise complaints, until early Wednesday morning, when Officers Jimmy Farlow and Amos Smith were summoned to the alley next to my favorite coffee shop. The poor girl who'd made the mistake of lifting the lid of the bin was being cared for inside.

~

I snagged a prime parking spot in front of Ava's Java, leapt out of the Chrysler, and jogged to the front door, arriving late to the early morning meeting of the Mentor Group. We were sort of a volunteer town council meeting regularly to discuss civic concerns, and to occasionally offer advice on affairs of the heart to anyone in need.

Ava, a founding member, reserved our table as long as we promised to get the meeting underway before the morning coffee rush. The other members of the Mentor Group would have been on time and taken their places at the only round table large enough to seat ten.

With my need for caffeine, and my eyes on the coffee counter, I barely glanced at my friends, but gave a shout. "The coffee smells great. Sorry I'm late. Pretty sure it was the cat again. Did I miss anything?"

The room was eerily silent. There were no cute comments, such as, "Nice of you to join us" and not even a loud dramatic sigh. I tore my gaze away from the carafe and glanced in the direction of the group. There were eight women's faces around the table, and not one of them wore the smile I'd expected. A few gazed in my direction without expression. Most sat with eyes lowered, studying the table.

I put on the brakes, causing my sneakers to squeak

on Ava's shiny tile floor. "What's going on?"

No response. I studied the group. Ava's waitress sat nestled among the other women, tears streaming. And there was a police officer, in the starched tan uniform, standing at attention nearby. I must have missed his squad car in my hurry.

"Hello, Officer Farlow." I tried to express the greeting without betraying dread. The officer and I had never communicated well. We'd lived on different wave lengths since the first month I'd moved home.

Farlow's piercing gaze lingered on me for only a moment before he snapped at Ava's husband. "Get over to the door and don't let anyone else in." I was tempted to jump to Konrad's defense. Was Farlow aware the man kindly took time off from his regular job, every Wednesday morning, to cover the coffee counter? This, just so we could have our meeting without interruption?

Before I could make a move, Farlow's stare returned and had me nailed in place.

At this time, several of my friends attempted to fill me in on the happenings of the morning. At least it seemed to be their intent. With all of them speaking at once, the words mashed together in a sort of alphabet soup.

Farlow put a stop to it with a thunderous, "Quiet!" The group fell silent.

"Lauren Halloren, are you a member of this, what's it called? Mentor group?"

I stood up straighter. "Yes, sir. I am."

"So, why are you just getting here? Where have you been?"

"Me? Home. I was home." Suddenly I was out of breath. "Overslept. My cat, Mason, must have stepped on the alarm and turned it off." I pulled away from Farlow's stare to search the worried faces of my friends. "What's going on?"

"I'll talk to you later, Halloren." Farlow ordered me to sit, so I scampered to the table and slid into a seat between Anita and Clair, my two best friends. They looked at me with wide eyes and pursed lips.

As soon as Farlow turned his attention to his notebook, Anita leaned close enough to whisper the news.

"You're kidding!" The words flew out before I had a chance to think about it. I clapped my hand over my mouth, as Farlow snapped a frown at me.

Stacy Lutz sat across the table. She planted her elbows on either side of a coffee cup and whispered, loudly. "You should have been here. You're the detective, after all. The body's still in the dumpster. Go out and take a look. I bet you can find some clues."

I slumped into my chair and whispered back at her. "I'm not a detective! I'm a writer and beauty shop receptionist. Just because I happened to find a killer or two—"

"Three." Stacy corrected.

I waved an index finger. "To be clear, I didn't know who killed the insurance man, until she broke into my house. And the mummy. I happened on to that by accident. Besides, it wasn't even a murder."

I looked to Clair for support but found her entranced by her cell phone. "What are you doing?"

Clair glanced at me. "I'm posting to my social media pages. Have to get this out there before anyone else." She returned to tapping her phone.

Anita shot her a look. "You're not posting about

the body."

"I sure am. This will be great for my Internet presence. That's how I promote my business. People will read this and click through to my real estate site. I'm always on the lookout for interesting topics. I bet I'll get a thousand clicks today."

With one last tap on her phone, Clair smiled. "If I want to build a following, I have to be active with intriguing news. Isn't that right, Gloria?"

The local librarian nodded her agreement. "Absolutely. We've been working on the library website. Gotta keep up with the times."

I blew out a breath and turned to Stacey. "Anyway, Clair had just as much to do with discovering dead bodies and murderers as I had."

"Whatever." Stacy performed an exaggerated eye roll. She did that often. I wondered if the young hairdresser had any control over her eyeballs. "You have to admit you have more experience than any of us." She tipped her head and shifted her gaze to the kitchen door. *Again with the eyeballs.* "Go out there and take a look."

"I'm not...." I twisted toward Rarity Peabody, owner of the Rare Curl. Surely she would support me.

My boss simply shrugged. "It might help. You are good at that sort of thing."

Officer Farlow's face blotched deep red. "Nobody gets up from this table until I'm finished with the interrogation. And nobody goes near that alley."

Ava harrumphed. "Jimmy, you don't have to yell. We're all here to help. Aren't we, ladies?" Heads bobbed around the table.

Farlow flipped a page in his notebook. "I'm going

to interview each one of you, so wait your turn to speak."

He focused his gaze on Melanie D'agostino, the waitress at Ava's Java. I'd first met Melanie a couple years earlier when she'd visited the Rare Curl, thinking she wanted to become a hairdresser. "I take it you found the body."

Melanie sank back into her chair and nodded. "Uh-huh."

"Full name?"

Rarity put an arm around Melanie. Never one to keep silent. "For goodness sakes Jimmy, you know who she is. Can't you see the girl is upset?"

Farlow raised his pen and glared. Rarity clamped her lips together.

He refocused his laser gaze on Melanie. "Full name?"

She sniffed. "My name is Melanie Maria D'agostino."

"Tell me about how you happened to find the body. Why were you in the alley so early this morning? Doesn't seem like a place a nice young girl would go."

Melanie grabbed a tissue and pressed it to her eyes.

Ava put a protective arm around the teenager. "Poor thing. She came in—"

Farlow scowled at the coffee shop owner. "Isn't Miss D'agostino able to speak for herself?"

Ava harrumphed. "Of course."

Farlow squared his shoulders and refocused on Melanie. "From the beginning."

The girl's eyes grew larger and more frightened. A blush crept from her neck to her pale cheeks.

Farlow maintained his steady gaze. "Speak up."

Melanie lifted a trembling hand and pointed in the direction of the kitchen. She stuttered, "I came in through the back door this morning so I could grab the trash from last night and take it out." Her thin shoulders shuddered. "When I lifted the lid of the garbage bin, I made the mistake of looking inside."

She closed her eyes and shook her head. "I don't usually, because it's smelly and full of gross stuff. But I looked, and...." She sucked in a deep breath and lifted a hand to her mouth. "A body. There was a body in there."

Rarity Peabody had been silent as long as any hairdresser could, under the circumstances. "I can tell you she was shocked. She let out a shriek that pierced the air all the way in here. Scared us all half to death. Even Konrad." She lifted her hand to point to Ava's husband. "Do you know Konrad Kraus? Anyway, he dropped a whole tray of cups. What a crash. Shattered mugs and spilled coffee all over the floor." Rarity scanned the floor around the counter. "See for yourself. I think there's still some broken glass under that table."

Konrad interrupted. "Your story's getting away from you, Rarity. The officer doesn't care about broken cups." He directed his gaze to Farlow. "Anyway, there was the scream, and nobody knew what the commotion was about."

Konrad turned toward the kitchen door as if he were visualizing the action. "Then Melanie came in, sort of staggered in, really." He demonstrated a stagger. "She just looked at us. I suppose it took her a minute to get her wits about her. Then she told us what she'd found." He twisted toward Farlow and shrugged. "Well I figured I had to go out to look. Clair and Anita went with me. And I think Irma."

The women nodded.

Irma chimed in. "Well, Jimmy, as a city employee, as soon as I saw it I called emergency services."

The policeman sputtered. "It's Officer Farlow. This is a crime scene."

This time, Irma rolled her eyes.

"Um, Officer Farlow?" Patricia Martin, local dress shop owner, attracted his attention. "When all this began, I didn't believe it. You know girls. So dramatic at this age. I thought for sure it was one of the old manikins from my shop. You know, a prank. When we threw them out, I half expected them to show up in the city park." She stifled a giggle. "But Clair went to look and said it was an actual corpse. And she's seen dead bodies before, so I took her word for it."

All of us, around the table, glanced at Clair and nodded our agreement. After all, she'd been the one to find a murdered man in the ravine a couple of years earlier. And the year after that she happened on a mummy in a house she was showing.

Rarity's red curls bobbed. "I appreciate you getting here as quickly as you did, Jimmy. This is so upsetting. I think I speak for all of us when I say we won't have a good night's sleep until you find out what happened to that poor man."

The policeman tapped his notebook. "Rest assured, I will get to the bottom of this." Farlow paused a moment before muttering, "And it's Officer Farlow."

Chapter Two

I flinched at the tap on my shoulder and turned to see Clair hovering there. She pointed to the front window. A dozen or more faces were pressed to the glass. "The crowd's getting mean. If it wasn't for Konrad, they'd probably storm the place. People don't like to be deprived of their caffeine."

Ava's husband stood guard, arms across his chest. He was not a tall man, a couple inches shorter than his wife, but his day job at the lumber company had developed imposing upper body strength. His stance made it clear no one dared try the door.

Konrad shot the mob a last look of warning before leaving his post to refill coffee mugs around our table. As he drew close to his wife, he muttered. "Don't worry, honey. At least it's no one we know."

Ava took his hand and gazed up at him. "Are you sure? You can't tell me you got a close look. You get queasy carving the roast beef."

"I saw enough. And I've got my antacids." He patted his shirt pocket.

"Besides, it's no one Clair or Anita recognized.

9

Between the two of them, they know about everyone in town."

Konrad glanced around the table, his gaze stopping with Rarity. "Come to think of it, as owner of the beauty shop, you have more history than anyone else, Mrs. Peabody. Maybe you should take a look."

"No." Rarity's red curls flew as she shook her head. "I'm sure Jimmy has everything under control." She looked up at the officer. "Jimmy, who is it? You can tell us. We'll promise to keep it quiet, if you say so."

Officer Farlow kept his eyes on his notebook. The muscles in his jaw flexed, and I thought I heard the grinding of teeth.

Konrad finished his round of refills and stepped close to Farlow. "Yeah, who is he? Did you know the guy?"

Farlow waved off the question. "Don't have an ID yet. I haven't seen the body. Officer Smith is in charge of the identification process."

Irma snickered and put her elbows on the table. She raised her eyebrows at me. "Jimmy's been shy about crime scenes ever since you found that mummy last year. I swear he was green for days, and I don't think he could eat a full meal for a week."

"Can't blame him." The memory of the smell still haunted my dreams.

Konrad eyed Farlow. "Are you telling me, Officer, you haven't even seen the dead man?"

Officer Farlow expanded his chest, or attempted to. "That's what I'm saying. We delegate responsibility at the department. Speaking of responsibility, I told you to guard the door. That mob gets in here, it's on you."

Farlow returned his attention to Melanie D'agostino and continued his interrogation. "The dead man. Did you know him?"

Melanie lowered her eyelids and shook her head. "No. It isn't like I got up close and stared at him. Soon as I saw the blood, I slammed the lid closed. Got away from there like a flash."

Farlow tapped his notebook. "Wait a minute. The name D'agostino rings a bell. Is your grandmother, Deloris D'agostino?"

Melanie nodded.

"She's incarcerated. For murder as I recall. And you were involved."

Rarity jumped out of her chair so fast she sent it scooting across the floor. Her index finger vibrated about an inch from the policeman's face. "Hold on one minute, Jimmy Farlow. This girl had nothing to do with that crime. She was only a child back then. How could she have known what her uncle and grandmother were up to? You know, perfectly well, she was exonerated of all charges."

Farlow let his menacing gaze linger on Melanie for a moment, before shifting it to Rarity. "That's correct. The judge said she was an unwitting participant. As far as I'm concerned, that only means there was a lack of evidence to the contrary. I'll be keeping an eye on her."

After scribbling in his notebook and flipping the page, the policeman pivoted to his left to face Ava. "Mrs. Kraus, what explanation do you have for the dead man ending up outside your shop? Anyone else use that dumpster?"

Ava raked her fingers through her hair. "No. I guess I'm the only one." She grabbed a napkin and dabbed at perspiration dotting her forehead. "Maybe it was someone who complained about my coffee. I don't remember killing anyone for that, lately."

Konrad was back at his wife's side in an instant. "That was a joke, Officer. She didn't mean it. She makes dumb comments when she's stressed."

Ava raised her eyes to the policeman. "I'm sorry. I don't think before I speak. It's been a rough day."

The back door creaked open and clanged shut, causing everyone in the room, including Officer Farlow, to jerk, and conversation to halt. We pivoted in unison, some of us likely expecting to see the murderer standing in the kitchen. To our relief, it was Amos Smith.

He sauntered into the room and smiled at everyone. "The body's been picked up and is on its way to the morgue. How's everybody doing? You okay, Melanie?" She didn't respond, but he gave her a pat on the shoulder.

He nodded to me. "Hi Ms. Halloren. Haven't seen you for a while."

I gave him a little wave. I'd always liked Amos. He was a big guy, sort of soft, not obviously muscular, but you felt safe in his presence. Polite and easy to talk to. He didn't strike me as the policeman type, more like an older brother or a favorite uncle.

At this point, I thought Jimmy Farlow might have wanted to explode, but he said, "Officer Smith, did you find any identification?"

Amos shoved his hand into his pocket. "Oh, yeah. Almost forgot. The victim's name is Giles Q. Gold. Driver's license out of New York state." He pulled out a brown leather billfold and offered it to his superior officer.

Farlow snatched the evidence from Amos's grasp and spun to face the group. Each of us received a probing gaze before he turned back to the older officer. "Amos, know any Golds?"

Amos shrugged and stuck his hands in his pockets. "Haven't heard the name around here."

Farlow studied the driver's license again, and then swiveled toward me. "Do you know the man?"

"No! I've never heard of him. Why are you asking me?"

"Seemed likely, you being from out of town."

"Am not. I'm from right here in Evelynton. I was gone for a while, but I've been back over four years." Farlow knew all this and I could tell he'd stopped listening.

He spun, once more, to face Ava. "Who is he?"

She shook her head. "I have no idea."

Farlow towered menacingly over Ava, which he could only do because she was sitting. Ava was taller than many of the men in town. "What are the chances a man's body was dumped right outside your back door, and you don't know him?"

Ava began to shake her head again. "I don't..." Her face paled. Brushing hair from her face, she said. "Oh my. The name is familiar. But it can't be him. The man I'm thinking of is a food critic. I don't actually know him, only read about him." She swung her gaze to Clair.

At that point, Clair let out a gasp and bounced up from her chair. "You're thinking of the Giles Gold who writes a blog called "Dissecting the Plate." But it can't be him. He won't be here until..." Clair's eyes grew large and her voice trailed off as she lowered herself into her seat.

Shifting his gaze from Ava to Clair, Farlow demanded, "Now we're getting somewhere. What do you know about the man?"

Clair's voice was barely above a whisper. "It's just that Giles Gold was the celebrity judge we recruited for the Marshmallow Festival cook off. We were counting on him to draw crowds from miles around."

Farlow's mouth dropped open. "The festival? That's weeks away. What was he doing in town, now?"

Ignoring Officer Farlow, Clair shifted her gaze to Ava. "It must be him."

Ava raised a hand to her mouth. "I guess you're right. How many men with that name could there be?"

Clair slowly shook her head. "This is a catastrophe. What are we going to do for a judge at such short notice? We need a celebrity."

Patricia Martin leaned in and hissed. "The Marshmallow Festival will be ruined. There's no time to find another big name from the food community. We're sunk."

Clair's forehead creased. "What do you think about the mayor? Maybe he would fill in. He probably has free time."

Irma flapped a hand. "That man doesn't know anything about food, except maybe barbecue."

I'm not usually one to assist Farlow. I prefer to keep out of his line of vision, but I could see he was floundering with this inquiry. I raised my voice. "Ladies. Dead man in the alley. Remember?"

Clair slumped into her seat. "Sorry, Lauren. You're right, of course. We'll discuss the festival at another time."

Farlow closed his eyes for a moment before commanding Officer Smith to take names and set appointments for us to give statements at the police station."

Having regained control, and using his best interrogative strategy, Officer Farlow stared into each woman's eyes, one by one. I thought he was trying to be certain he had our attention. Or he might be trying to burn holes into our consciousness. I glanced away when it was my turn to receive his threat.

"Every one of you is a suspect. I think the killer is in this room and I won't stop until I discover who it is."

After this announcement, the officer straightened and let his eyes roam the group one more time. "This is your last chance. What do you know about Giles Q. Gold? What connection does he have with Ava's Java? Or is the connection with one of you? It will go easier for you if you confess now."

Jimmy Farlow studied each face. I couldn't help but do the same. Could someone at this table—one of my friends—be a murderer?

Chapter Three

I was relieved to see the backs of Officers Farlow and Smith. I watched through the window as they crossed the sidewalk and climbed into their squad car. As soon as they sped away, the members of our mentor group quickly dispersed. Everyone had errands to run or work to do, and tales to tell. Rarity and I lingered, gathering used cups and napkins.

Ava hadn't moved from her seat at the table. I doubt she could summon enough energy to rise from her chair.

Rarity nudged Konrad. "You go on to work. We'll finish cleaning up." She grabbed a rag and began wiping the table.

Konrad removed his apron, folded and tucked it into a drawer. From there he went to his wife's side and pulled her into a hug. "What's going on? I know this has been traumatic, but you aren't yourself. You're holding something back. Are you sure you didn't know that Giles character?"

Ava answered him, but spoke too quietly for me to hear.

I've always hated whispering. I don't know why I think I should be privy to everything that's said, but telling myself it's not my business, has never helped curtail my curiosity. I find myself leaning in and straining to make out each muttered word.

So of course, I grabbed a broom and found some crumbs on the floor near the table.

"No, I did not know him." Ava paused, averting her eyes. "Well not really. I met him once at a conference. He even bought me a drink, but that was all. I was flattered. We talked about the Java. The truth is, he seemed a little too interested, so I cut the evening short and went to my room. I didn't attend any of his talks the next day."

Konrad shook his head. "My love, you lied to the police."

"I was scared. Don't know why I didn't tell the truth, but after the first denial, I was afraid to change my story. I knew they'd hold that against me. They always do on television."

Ava shot a glance at me. I concentrated on sweeping the floor, pretending I hadn't heard and wasn't dying to hear more.

Konrad kissed her on the cheek. "I wish you would sell the shop and retire. You're carrying too much stress."

Ava drew back and blinked at her husband. "What are you saying? I love this place."

Konrad laid a large hand on Ava's cheek. "Yes, I know you do. I'm sorry I mentioned it. Anyway, tell Officer Farlow the whole truth, tomorrow."

Ava kissed his hand. "I will. I promise. You go to work and don't worry about me."

At this point, I'd begun to feel like a voyeur, and looked for something else to do.

Konrad left by the front door, scowled at the remaining few gawkers on the sidewalk, and pointed at the closed sign still hanging in the window.

Rarity deposited her rag in the sink and hustled over to sit next to Ava. "The dishes are all cleaned up, so Lauren and I will be going now. Stacie's probably ready for some help at the salon. We can thank the Lord the worst is over. The police will find an explanation for this."

I put the broom away, waved at Ava and waited for Rarity by the door.

My boss was one of those people whose good-bye could last longer than the original visit. She got up from the table and made it half-way to the door before she thought of more to say. "It's awful something like that happened next to the Java, but we all know the man had no connection to you. I'm sure this will be cleared up before you know it. Um, is there anything else we can do?"

Ava pushed up from her chair. "You've already done enough. I can take it from here. Best to get on with my day. I just want to open the shop and let life return to normal."

Rarity made it to the door before hesitating again. She gripped the closed sign. "Are you sure you want to open today? Why don't you take the day off?"

"I can't do that. Look out on the sidewalk." Ava held out her hands to the clusters of towns-people gathering once again.

She slid her chair under the table and smoothed her apron. "No. I'll feel fine once I begin working."

Rarity leaned on the door, her back to the probing eyes of her neighbors. "Did I hear Konrad say something about you retiring?"

Ava snapped to attention. "Me retire? He mentioned it, but he wasn't thinking clearly. What would I do with myself if I didn't have the Java? It's like you, if you didn't have The Rare Curl. Except you would probably be involved in all sorts of charity work. This is all I have."

She strode to the center of the shop and smiled—almost beamed. "Ava's Java is the hub of the community. If something's going on, you'll hear it here first." She glanced at the customer faces peering through the window, and lowered her voice. "People think they're talking privately, but I hear everything. That's how I know who needs help and who needs my prayers. As long as I serve the coffee, they don't pay attention to me. I'm the invisible woman."

Rarity folded her arms, exhibiting no desire to leave.

I followed my boss's example and folded my arms. I had a question of my own. "That brings up a question. What if the murderer has been in the Java? You may have heard something you don't even remember. Something that might incriminate them. What if they think you might know who they are?"

Ava sputtered a laugh. "Not a chance. I'd know if there was a murderer in my shop. These are my people. And now, with the Mentor Group, I have a chance to do some good for my town. Life is just beginning for me."

The door behind Rarity vibrated. She planted her feet and glanced over her shoulder. "Shall I turn the sign?"

"Yes. Open the door." Ava grinned. "Let my people in."

Rarity flipped the sign over. A cheer could be heard outside, and people began pushing on the door even before we jumped out of the way.

A line soon formed at the coffee counter, taking Ava's full attention. Rarity and I slipped out.

I wondered if they were truly Ava's people. Did they all appreciate the good woman who served them coffee? Or was one of them plotting to silence a possible witness to a murder?

Chapter Four

My rearview mirror showed Stacey Lutz, in her spiffy new Chevy Spark, tailing me into the parking lot. I wondered if I would ever choose a raspberry colored car. Providing I ever had an opportunity to actually choose a color, or a car? My '75 Chrysler New Yorker station wagon, avocado with wood toned panels down the side, had come to me as an inheritance from Aunt Ruth.

Stacey popped out of her shiny little car and slung her bag over her shoulder. She waited for me to wrestle open the heavy door of the Chrysler and to push down all the locks. I gave the door a shove, silently apologizing to my aunt, who always said, "You don't have to slam the door. It's a Chrysler."

I joined Stacey on the walk to the salon. "How was your interview with Farlow, yesterday? Did they keep you forever?"

Knowing Jimmy Farlow as I did, I expected a horror story. Stacey giggled. "It was a breeze. Officer Farlow was much too busy to worry about me, so Amos took my statement." She waved a hand and snapped her fingers. "I signed it and was out of there in about two minutes. Amos was really sweet and assured me he always knew when someone was telling the truth. And he believed me."

She grinned. "I'd always thought he judged me for my hair. You know, the color and funky cut, but I guess not." My purple haired coworker glanced at me. "How did it go for you?"

"You were lucky. Farlow interrogated me for more almost an hour and repeated every question at least three times. My guess is he wanted to catch me off guard, but I could hardly forget the answer I'd just given—twice. He finally gave up and let me sign my statement. I suspect it was time for his lunch."

Stacey and I crossed the street and stood at the door. My salon keys seemed to be perpetually lost, somewhere at the bottom of my handbag. I'd been searching since we left the parking lot and still came up empty handed.

"Let me get it." Stacey stepped ahead of me and pushed her key into the door.

Once inside, she trudged to her styling station to deposit her bag, and I aimed for the reception desk.

My coworker pulled out a curling iron and pointed it at me. "Let me tell you, it's a good thing you're working today. If I had to answer that phone one more time to hear 'What happened at Ava's?' 'Tell me about the dead man.' or 'Who do you think did it?', I would scream. It rang constantly yesterday. I wouldn't have minded if the calls were for appointments."

Now, the Stacey I knew would have yearned to share her first-hand knowledge, elaborating and speculating on the crime.

"And that was a problem?"

Stacey planted her hands on her hips and gave me a look. "Think about it. Everyone knows Rarity's rule about no gossip in the salon." She blew out a breath and pointed toward Rarity's empty styling station. "She was right there working, all day. How could I say anything?"

Flopping into her styling chair, Stacey ran her fingers through her bangs. "Anyway, I kept telling them I didn't know anything, and I was sure the police department would solve it very soon. I sounded just like Rarity."

She swiveled her chair to face me. "They probably thought I'd lost my mind."

"You showed commendable self-control. I'm sure Rarity appreciated it."

The motto at The Rare Curl was well known. I glanced up at the quotation Rarity had stenciled above the waiting room door. It read: **Fix your thoughts on what is true, and honorable, and right, and pure, and lovely, and admirable. Think about things that are excellent and worthy of praise. Philippians 4:8**

"I'm glad you reminded me. I might have been drawn in to conversations about the murder. Mind if I use your answer so everyone gets the same story?"

As if on cue, the phone rang. I snatched it from the cradle, fully prepared with an answer to any non-business related question. "Good morning. It's a beautiful day at The Rare Curl."

"Hey, Lauren. It's Irma. Stacey got any time for a haircut, today?"

I scanned the appointment book. "She does if you get here soon. Can you make it in twenty minutes?"

"I'm on my way."

I replaced the handset. "I just filled your opening this morning. Irma."

"From the police station?"

At my nod, Stacey grabbed her styling cape and flipped open the folds, letting a smile play across her face. "What time does Rarity start work today?"

"Not until noon." I tried to give my coworker a stern look. "I want nothing to do with prying information from Irma. Just because the boss isn't here, doesn't mean we break the rule."

Stacey shook her head vigorously. "Wouldn't even think of it. Of course if Irma brings it up and wants to talk, it wouldn't be nice to ignore her. That would be rude." Stacy lifted her feet, and spun her chair. "Bet it won't take five minutes for her to come out with some interesting information. That woman loves to talk about police business."

I put my hands over my ears. "I won't listen."

The little bells on the front door jingled. My friend Anita held the door open and leaned in. "Are you busy? I was in town and thought I'd drop by for a chat."

"Come on in. No customers in here yet. I have nothing to do but wait for the phone to ring."

Anita grabbed a chair from the waiting area and dragged it to the side of my desk. "So what have you heard about the corpse?"

"Not a thing."

She stared at me. "Nothing?"

I clapped a hand over my mouth and pointed to Rarity's motto.

Anita squinted at me. "But you can tell me. You know I won't spread it around."

"I really haven't heard anything. But if I did, it wouldn't be right to talk about it at work."

"Darn. I'm dying to know why the man was in town. What do you think we should do? Maybe check around at the motels to discover where he was staying?"

"Once again, Rarity's rule is no speculating about it in the salon. And we aren't going to do anything. The authorities are more than capable."

Anita's rosy cheeks drooped into a pout. "Gosh, you're no fun at all. I might as well go home."

Stacey's voice drifted in from the styling area. "Did you tell Anita Irma is going to be here, for a haircut, in fifteen minutes? I sure hope she doesn't want to talk about the murder."

I was about to warn the two inquisitive women about the ramifications of gossip, when the phone rang.

After taking a message and replacing the handset I noticed Anita was no longer beside my desk. She sat in the waiting area, seemingly entranced by a Vogue magazine. She glanced at me over the top of the page. "I haven't seen this issue. Mind if I stick around and read it?"

"Not at all." Apparently, I had no control over the situation.

Ten minutes later, the doorbells jingled and Irma arrived. She waved as she passed through the waiting room. "Hi Anita, how's it going?"

Anita gave a little wave and returned to reading, or pretending to.

Irma tapped my desk on her way to Stacey's styling chair. "Hey, Halloren. What's up?"

"Nice to see you, Irma. Would you care for coffee?" Excelling in my receptionist role.

"No thanks." Irma hopped into the chair where Stacey waited with styling cape ready to settle around her shoulders.

Stacey kept her promise and refrained from asking about the crime. Not a difficult feat, since Irma couldn't wait to regale us with recent police activities. Information bubbled from her as bits of hair flew to the floor. "You should see Jimmy Farlow strut around the station. Since Chief Stoddard went on leave and left him in charge, you'd think he was Sherlock Holmes"

I studied the appointment book, but shifted to point an ear in Irma's direction. Anita slid into a chair closer to the styling area.

Stacey muttered. "What's Farlow think?"

"Well, he says he's positive it wasn't a coincidence the food critic ended up dead outside Ava's Java."

Anita popped out of her seat and scampered to hover over Irma. "I hope he's not blaming Ava. She doesn't know anything about it."

"Sorry to say he's looking at Ava as a suspect. But there's also that girl, Melanie. He doesn't believe she is completely innocent."

With fists planted on her hips, Anita played defense. "We all know it couldn't be either one of them. They are nice people."

Irma shrugged. "You might be right, but as Officer Farlow always says, you don't know what a person is capable of, given the proper motivation."

"I'll never believe it of either of them. What else do you know?"

Irma shifted her head toward Anita, causing Stacey to fumble her comb. "The doc reported Gold was killed by repeated blows to the head. He said there was a sticky substance in the wounds."

Stacey retrieved another comb from the drawer. "Ick. Something sticky besides blood?"

"He sent it to be tested, but figured it was cookie dough. So he says that might be the murder weapon. Isn't that nuts?"

Stacey stopped trimming and faced Irma. "Cookie dough? That's crazy. How could anyone be hurt by cookie dough?"

Irma laughed. "Even Farlow didn't believe that one. And he'll fall for about anything. Those doctor types think just because they've been to medical school, they know everything. If you ask me, he's educated beyond his intelligence."

Stacy picked up a spray bottle and gave Irma's hair a mist. "I'm glad to hear Jimmy is thinking for himself. But I don't believe Ava would hurt anyone."

"Hate to break it to you, but Ava looks like the culprit. I shouldn't say anything, me being a city official, but it'll be common knowledge soon. Ava changed her story when she went in to give her statement yesterday. Bet you didn't know she was acquainted with the victim."

Stacey dropped her shears. "What?"

Anita gaped. "No."

I couldn't keep my mouth shut any longer. Ava needed defending. "Ava was nervous and spoke without thinking when she denied knowing Gold. Then she was afraid to change her answer."

Anita and Stacey pivoted in unison to glare at me. Stacey sputtered. "You knew about this?"

It took Anita a minute to speak. "Why didn't you tell me, your friend and fellow detective?"

Crap. I was in trouble now. Anita looked stricken, as if I'd broken a sacred oath. Stacey might never talk to me again. And the way Irma squinted at me, I thought she'd be calling the authorities at any moment.

"Let me explain." The three women focused on me. "When all members of the mentor group had left, except Rarity and me, I overheard a conversation between Ava and Konrad. I couldn't repeat it, it was private. Do you understand?" I searched Anita's face, who appeared to grasp my innocent intent. I averted my eyes from Stacey, who showed no sign of grace.

To Irma, I said, "Ava promised Konrad she would confess her mistake to Farlow, so I saw no reason to report it.

Anita twisted back to Irma. "I'm sure Ava had a good reason for what she did. We all know her like family. She's lived here forever."

Irma shrugged. "You think you know someone, but how well? Anyone can put up a good front. But one day that pretty facade slips to reveal the monster underneath."

Stacey pressed her lips together and wrinkled her brow while she continued to trim Irma's hair.

Irma went on. "Maybe you're correct and Ava is okay, but what about that husband of hers? Does anyone really know him? I only met him when he started showing up at the weekly mentor meetings." She glanced at Anita. "Did you ever meet him before that?"

Anita gave a small shake of her head. "No. But he's a good man. Look how nice he's been, watching the counter so we aren't interrupted. He loves Ava, and he's interested in the success of our mentor group."

Irma raised an index finger. "I agree he loves Ava. To what lengths would he go if he thought someone was going to hurt his wife, or maybe write a bad review of her precious coffee shop?"

Anita ran both hands through her hair. "This is so distressing. I can't believe Konrad would do that."

Since my earlier outburst, I'd determined to stay in my chair and keep my mouth shut, but I wanted to defend Konrad, too. The door bells drew my attention, and I twisted to see Rarity coming through the front door. Saved from breaking Rarity's no gossip rule, I spun my chair back to the desk.

Rarity's auburn curls bounced as she strode past. "Hi Irma. I love the new short haircut. Pixie cuts are adorable."

Irma glanced at her reflection in the mirror, and did a double-take.

It's a good thing hair grows. Irma's problem would solve itself in a couple of months. Would the murder be solved as easily?

Chapter Five

I don't actually remember agreeing to this meeting." I trailed Clair into Ava's Java, still sleepy from being dragged out of bed earlier than I'd planned. Clair, an eternally early riser, assumed everyone followed her example.

"Of course you did. I said, 'Mentor meeting in ten minutes.' And you said, 'Okay.'"

As I recalled it, after she banged on my door to get me up, she said 'Get in your car and meet me at Ava's Java.' I was too groggy to resist and knew there would be coffee.

Clair deposited her handbag on the first table inside the door and pulled out her cell phone. "We have business to discuss."

I silently thanked the Lord our meetings were held at Ava's and directed my feet to the coffee counter where a full carafe was waiting.

Anita, Rarity and Patricia ambled in a minute later, smiles and attire suggesting they'd been up for hours.

Rarity said, "It's wonderful we were all able to meet again."

Clair shrugged. "Not everyone. Stacey and Irma didn't answer their phones. I left each of them a message, but don't see a reply."

Patricia glanced at the table Ava had prepared for us. "What about Gloria, from the library? I haven't seen her for a while."

"She's been busy with some project, but I'm keeping her updated. So let's get started. We haven't much time to construct promotions for the Marshmallow Festival. Our meeting on Wednesday was a disappointment. We didn't accomplish anything."

Anita, who wasn't one to roll her eyes, did. "Yes, wasn't it inconvenient that a man died in Ava's dumpster?"

Patricia picked up an empty mug from the counter and passed it to Anita. "I feel terrible about the death, too. But we business owners have to keep an eye on the bottom line. I, for one, depend on additional income from the festival."

Clair grabbed the next mug. "That's right. Since we haven't had the festival in the last few years, it's important we make this one a success. It benefits the whole town."

I didn't think I could develop interest in the bottom line until after my morning coffee, so I filled a cup with Ava's Bombshell Blend, and moved to the side. With the first heartwarming sip, I glanced through the front door. "Oh crap. Look who's coming."

My friends pivoted to gaze through the window. Officers Farlow and Smith strode across the sidewalk, exuding a determined and authoritative air. Once inside, Farlow took up space directly in front of the coffee counter. "Everyone out. I'm shutting this place down until we search it.

Sometimes, or to be honest, many times, I forget to sort my thoughts before they shoot out of my mouth in verbal form. "You've got to be kidding. You're doing this today? What kind of police work is that? The crime scene is cold by now. It seems to me you should have done your search on the day of the crime, or the day after at the latest, when evidence was fresh. In all the books I've read, they…."

Farlow speared me with a gaze that caused the tirade to die in my throat. "We know what we're doing, Halloren. We are the police department and we are searching today. Interfere once more and you'll find us searching your residence this afternoon."

I scooted back a few inches. "My house? Why? I didn't have anything to do with this." Farlow continued to stare at me until I mumbled. "Ladies, I think we should find another place to meet this morning."

Rarity didn't intimidate so easily. "This is so inconvenient, Jimmy. How long will your business take?"

Farlow planted one hand on his holstered weapon. "It will take as long as it takes to do a thorough sweep of the place. And then, as long as it takes me to consider the evidence we collect."

At Farlow's signal, Amos Smith pulled the door open. My friends began to file out.

Ava lingered, wringing her hands. "Evidence? You aren't going to find anything in my shop. I've told you everything."

Farlow nailed her with his glare. "If you're telling the truth—this time—our job should be easy. But understand this, the longer you stand there impeding my investigation, the longer this coffee shop will be shut down."

I put an arm around Ava and walked with her to the sidewalk where the rest of the group congregated. For a large woman, Ava seemed particularly frail as she faced her friends. "I have an apology to make. You see, this is all my fault. When I went in to make my statement at the police station, I admitted, to the officer, I lied about knowing Giles Gold.

Struck speechless, Clair and Patricia swiveled in her direction.

Ava took a breath and spit out her explanation. "I met him once. That's all. And I don't know why I didn't admit it the first time Officer Farlow asked. But the meeting with Giles was so brief, I forgot."

She dipped her chin and shook her head slightly. "No. That's not true. I didn't forget. I'd never told Konrad about the incident. Thought he might be jealous." Ava glanced at Rarity and took a deep breath. "I couldn't tell the police in front of my husband, after having kept him in the dark."

We all nodded our understanding. I couldn't help but think of another of Aunt Ruth's sayings. Something about a tangled web and deceit.

Ava seemed to take encouragement and continued. "When the police left, I told him. Of course he insisted I confess to the authorities."

Rarity hugged her. "Konrad is a good man. Was he angry?"

"Not at all. I'd been silly. He was sweet and understanding."

Patricia lowered her voice and leaned close to Ava. "Just how well did you know Gold? Um. In what sense?"

Ava didn't make any attempt to lower her voice. "Not in any sense! I met him once at the convention. He seemed a bit forward, so I stayed away from the rest of his lectures. That was the end of it."

Rarity cut in. "Come ladies. Let's get off the sidewalk. We'll have our meeting at The Rare Curl, since it's right next door."

Ava straightened her shoulders. "You all go ahead. I'll stay here in case the officers need to talk to me. Maybe that will hurry things along. I don't know what I'll do if I can't open for the lunch rush."

She returned to the Java, while the rest of us trailed into the salon and took seats in the waiting room. I still cradled my mug of Ava's Bombshell Blend, with only a tinge of guilt that no one else had thought to get theirs. But the guilt was enough to prompt me to get up and start the salon coffee pot brewing.

A soft brush on my ankle brought my attention to the purring fluff ball on the floor. Peering up at me were the golden eyes of my cat, Mason. I'm not sure I should call him mine. Mason was a willful animal who had pretty much forced his way into my home and my heart not long after I moved into the house I'd inherited from my aunt. "What are you doing here?"

He emitted a soft "Mew," spun and leapt into an empty chair.

"Look. How did Mason know we'd be here? And he walked all the way." Clair pulled out her cell phone and snapped a picture. Then she scooted closer and leaned in to garner a selfie.

I eyed Clair. "Why would you take a selfie with my cat?"

"It'll be great for my social media pages. I'll call it 'Cat Joins Mentor Group.' Or 'Feline Wisdom.'"

Patricia glared at Mason, and glanced up at Rarity. "What's he doing here? Are animals allowed in beauty salons?" She examined her skirt and brushed off a few imaginary hairs.

Rarity smiled. "I love kitties. And isn't he cute? I'd have a salon resident cat, if I could. Mason can stay until we open the salon for customers, then Lauren will take him home."

Rarity filled Styrofoam cups with coffee and distributed them. When she came to me, with my mug from Ava's, she raised her eyebrows and moved on. She said to the group, "I hope you like the coffee. It isn't Ava's Java, but it's hot."

I wrapped my hands around my mug filled with the best stimulant in northern Indiana, hoping to cover the insignia.

We'd taken our seats, waiting for the meeting to begin when the door jingled open and Irma trotted in carrying her own travel mug. "Hi groupies. Figured you'd be here. Amos informed me of the Java search. I delayed, so as not to be caught in the middle of it."

Patricia's mood hadn't improved. "I think you could have let the rest of know. It was embarrassing. They walked in and evicted us."

Irma took a seat. "If I had, I'd got myself fired. You know, I don't talk about police business."

Anita shifted her gaze to me and whispered. "Oh no. Never."

Clair raised her voice above the chatter. "We're running a little late, so let's begin. What were we talking about at the last meeting, um, before we were interrupted?" This was Clair's version of not being bossy. She already knew the answer and had the agenda in mind.

Patricia obliged. "As I recall, the last question was how we can get more visitors to town, now that we don't have a celebrity judge."

She scanned the group with a smile that lacked sincerity. "To some, the topic may not seem particularly important, but we business owners depend on the increased income of the festival. We've already spent money preparing for it, and now we don't have a main attraction."

Patricia stood and took on somber tone. "I think I speak for all of us in saying we're all sorry that poor man turned up dead in the garbage bin. Maybe we'll have some sort of memorial for him. We can talk about that later, but now let's think about practical matters."

Irma took a long and noisy slurp of coffee. "I'll tell you a practical matter. There's a killer on the loose and we don't know who it is. Who do we trust? Hate to talk behind anyone's back, but the police think it's Ava, or Konrad, or that waitress, Melanie."

She twisted to face me. "Which one do you see as a criminal type, Halloren?"

I choked on my coffee. After I finished coughing, I squeaked. "Don't ask me. I don't know anyone with a murderous personality. I'm not even sure what that would look like. Anyway, Farlow's mistaken. Ava, Konrad, and Melanie are our friends. I think he will discover it's some unknown person. Maybe a stranger from out of town."

Irma chimed in. "That's right. Gold was from New York. What if the killer followed him here?"

Anita stood at the coffee bar pouring sugar into her cup. "And what if he's still in town? A homicidal maniac roaming the streets. Or a serial killer. Gang initiation? Do we have gangs in Evelynton?"

Rarity got up from her chair and stomped to the reception desk, where she used a hairbrush to rap on the glass top. The cat leapt from his chair, and everyone else gazed, with wide eyes, at the salon owner. "Ladies, we are here as the Mentor Group, and that requires helpful, encouraging, and constructive conversation. Let's abide by my salon motto." She pointed to the verse on the wall.

Mason peaked out from under a dryer chair. The rest of us quieted and looked sheepish. We spent the remainder of the hour discussing avenues of promotion for the Marshmallow Festival. Mostly Clair, Rarity, and Patricia discussed it. After which, they assigned us each a project to work on.

With that, the meeting was adjourned.

I'd leaned down to gather Mason from his hiding place when Anita snagged me. "I'll walk you to your car." She held the door as I juggled the squirming cat. "I'm sure you agree Farlow has made up his mind and won't investigate any further than Ava and Konrad. Or maybe Melanie. If we're going to save them from being falsely accused, you and I have to do something. And if Clair can stop worrying about her social media pages long enough, I'm sure she'll help."

We crossed the parking lot to the Chrysler, and I deposited Mason on the front seat, where he sat up to look out the window.

Anita stood for a moment watching traffic on Main Street. "How could this happen? We grew up here. Roamed the streets and were never afraid."

Shifting her gaze to me, Anita shook her head. "The atmosphere of our little town has changed. It's as though a shadow has settled over it."

We both shivered as a cloud chose that moment to blot out the sun.

Chapter Six

I replaced the receiver with relief. Nearly every phone call, this morning, had been legitimate. I actually did my job arranging hair appointments.

The front door swung open to the tune of jingling bells as Gladys, our cleaning lady clamored in. Her rolling mop bucket trailed behind her, piled high with mops and squeegees.

"Good morning, Lauren. I hoped you wouldn't mind me being in this morning. With the festival coming up, I've been getting calls for extra cleaning. Thought I'd get your windows done while I had the chance."

"Come on in. No one's going to complain about clean windows."

She leaned toward me as she unloaded her mops. "You were in the Java the other day when they found the dead guy, weren't you?"

"Yes. Well, sort of. I missed the big event. Got there right after." I didn't need to explain. She wasn't listening.

Gladys shook her head and squirted cleaning fluid into the bucket. "It's a terrible thing, leaving someone's body in a dumpster. It's disgraceful the way people behave. I can't believe all the crime in the world today."

Thinking of Rarity, I nodded and kept my lips pressed together. The gossip mill didn't need me to add fuel to the discussion. Given encouragement, Gladys would talk the entire time she worked. This would double the hours spent in the salon.

The woman rolled her bucket to the shampoo bowl to fill. "It's not just the killings. In general, people have no respect for the property of others. Always using things that don't belong to them, as if they had a right." She shook her head and turned on the water. "Take that very dumpster—"

The blessed telephone interrupted Gladys's monologue. I breathed a sigh of relief and answered. "It's a lovely morning at The Rare Curl. How can we make your day?" I'd been trying out new encouraging greetings.

A hoarse whisper came through the line. "Lauren, it's Ava. Don't have time to explain. I could use some back-up over here."

I hung up the phone and trotted to the supply room to find Rarity. "Ava needs help at the shop. I don't know what's going on but it sounded serious."

"I'm free. I'll go." Rarity wiped her hands on a towel and hustled to the door, greeting Gladys on the way out.

I was left to stew about the activity next door. Two would be better than one, as backup, wouldn't it?

"Gladys, hold down the fort. I'll be back in a few minutes."

"No problem. I can handle it here. When I was younger, I wanted to be a beautician. Even did my sister's hair."

I stopped with my hand on the door, and glanced back at the chatty woman. "If the phone rings, let it go to voice mail. If someone comes in, ask them to take a seat and tell them I'll be right back."

I caught up with Rarity, and we walked into the Java together.

Ava stood next to the counter surrounded by tears, squeals, and sobbing. I counted three individuals, spewing emotions, and taking up a lot of space.

Ava's relief was evident when she spied us. "My friends. Come and meet the family of that poor man who died."

She put a hand on the arm of a rotund woman with a mass of hair the color and the texture of old straw. The older woman stood a good four inches shorter than Ava, but may have outweighed her by twenty pounds. "Mrs. Ophelia Gold, these are my friends. They were here that dreadful day."

The lady stared at each of us and sniffed. "How do you do?"

I didn't know how to answer that question. Definitely better than she was doing. I said, "Hello."

Ava went on to introduce Gold's tearful daughter, Rosemary. She wasn't quite the size of her mother but would have been called pudgy, if someone wasn't being kind. She wore her blond hair pulled back severely, and formed into a bun at the back of her head. The third in the noisy trio turned out to be the son, Sage. The portly young man stood a bit taller than his mother and sister, and was considerably rounder. His hairstyle assumed the shape of a donut, beginning above the ears, and ending in a bare spot on top of his head.

I can't say exactly when I began describing everyone by hairstyle, but I suppose it was soon after I became the receptionist at The Rare Curl. Hair was now first on the list of traits I noticed in people.

Rarity reached into the circle to grab Mrs. Gold's hand. "Dear Mrs. Gold, I've wanted to convey my sympathy to you and your children, but didn't know how to contact you. And here you are. Let me express how sorry we all are for your loss. How can we be of service during this difficult time?" I should have been taking notes. Rarity always said the right thing.

The Gold family didn't respond to sympathy in the way I'd expected. Sage Gold pulled out a handkerchief and wiped his nose. "The only service we're interested in is justice for the murder of my father."

Mrs. Gold dropped Rarity's hand and focused on Ava. The barista took a step back to avoid a pointing finger. Ophelia growled. "We've traveled a long way to discover what my husband was doing in such a place. What purpose would he have in visiting this...hamlet?"

Rarity smiled. "Didn't you know? He'd consented to be our celebrity judge for a festival we're having. Such an honor for us."

Rosemary Gold had been sobbing, but seemed to be trying to overcome her grief. She gave a somewhat hysterical laugh. "He's much too important to waste his time judging anything in a burg this size."

Mrs. Gold planted her hands in the vicinity of her copious hips, and studied Ava. "I'm beginning to understand. Giles was a brilliant man, but he had his weaknesses. He could be swayed by feminine wiles." She paused to scan Ava, head to toe. "I'm willing to bet you threw yourself at him, and being just the kind of tall, slim woman he would fall for, he couldn't help himself."

"Slim?" Ava glanced at her reflection in the display case and sucked in her stomach. Turning her attention back to the irate woman, she looked down at her. "First of all, Mrs. Gold, I assure you I didn't know your husband, let alone try to seduce him. There was nothing going on between us. Even if I was single, which I'm not," raising her left hand and displaying a worn wedding band, "I wouldn't have anything to do with a married man."

Rarity slid forward until she'd wedged herself between Ophelia Gold and Ava. "I know this is a stressful time for you all. Won't you have a nice cup of coffee? Ava's Java is known, far and wide, for their full-bodied decaf."

Rosemary sniffed. "Do you have espresso?"

Ophelia pulled a handful of tissues from her handbag. "We have no time for coffee. My children and I are here solely to see justice is done. We've heard how it works in these small towns. You'll sweep the crime under the rug to protect your own. Someone will pay for this. If necessary, I plan to take care of it myself."

Rarity stepped to a nearby table and pulled out a chair. In the soft, soothing voice, only my boss could muster, she said, "I can see you are distraught. Let us take care of you while you rest here. Coffee? Maybe a sweet roll?" Mrs. Gold sank into the chair and Rarity took a seat beside her. "I have faith, and God assures us, that right will be accomplished." She glanced up at Ava, who placed a plate of muffins on the table. Rarity continued. "The Evelynton police force is very conscientious, and you may be confident they will do everything in their power to catch the culprit."

"We don't want your coffee or sweet rolls." Mrs. Gold popped up from the table. "I see I'm getting nowhere. Come Sage. Rosemary, we don't have time for this. Off to the police station."

Sage reluctantly withdrew his hand from the tray of muffins and followed his mother and sister to the door. I waved to their backs. "Nice to meet you. Once again, I'm sorry for your loss. Goodbye Mrs. Gold, Sage, Rosemary."

It seemed Giles Gold was a womanizer. That was not good news. I didn't want to believe it, but could Ava have succumbed to flirtations of the famous food blogger? Was she the reason he'd traveled to our minuscule town?

Chapter Seven

L ater that afternoon, Clair, Anita, and I occupied the best table in Ava's Java, next to the widow, affording a clear view of Main Street. The coffee shop was filled, but quiet. I guess it was easy for Evelynton citizens to forget a murder had taken place— or at least to put it out of their minds, in favor of more pleasant topics.

Not so with Clair and Anita. They grilled me about the Golds.

"They were an emotional family. The crying was understandable, but a moment later, the tears stopped and they started yelling at Ava. Even Rarity's magical composure didn't get through to them. The three finally marched off to the police station. I wonder how Officer Farlow handled them."

Anita stirred sugar into her coffee. "To bad Irma's not here this morning. I bet she'd tell us all about their visit."

Clair's gaze darted to the coffee counter. "I see someone who might be just as interesting to talk to as Irma."

She swiveled in her chair and raised her voice

above the hum of conversation. "Amos Smith, we don't see you in here often."

The big man glanced at us, paid for his coffee and thanked Ava, before ambling over. He stood beside our table holding his to-go cup. "Hi, ladies. I've had enough stale coffee, from the station, to last me. Needed some of the good stuff."

Anita smiled. "How's work going?"

He shrugged. "Jimmy's had us working round the clock. He's determined to solve this case before Chief Stoddard gets back from vacation. That'd be a feather in his cap."

Amos took a sweeping glance around the coffee shop and lowered his voice. "The family of the deceased, coming to town, didn't help. They were blubbering and putt'n up a fuss one minute, and threatening to take it to the papers or call the governor, the next. That just added to Farlow's obsession."

Clair patted an empty chair at our table. "Why don't you sit with us and relax a few minutes? You deserve a rest." Amos probably didn't suspect, but I knew Clair had an ulterior motive for the invitation, beyond the deputy's need for relaxation.

A smile engulfed the man's face. "That would be nice." Amos settled into the chair and slumped over his coffee, cradling the cardboard cup.

Anita blessed him with a sweet smile. "You do seem tired. Are you feeling okay?"

"I've been better. This is a tough case. As I said, we've been putting in extra hours, so I haven't been home much. The wife's upset about it."

Anita's face crinkled. "I bet she misses you being home."

Amos nodded. "She does, but it's part of the job. She knew I wouldn't have regular hours when I joined the force."

Considering Evelynton's history of mostly petty crime, I doubted Mrs. Smith expected her husband's job to put much of a strain on their relationship.

Amos concentrated on his coffee for a few quiet moments, before he returned his attention to us. "Has the Mentor Group gotten back to regular meetings? I might come by to ask for some domestic advice. You all were helpful the last time I stopped in."

Clair shrugged. "Right now, we're trying to get the Marshmallow Festival underway. It's been a mess since our main attraction fell through. You might want to hang on until after that so we can devote our full attention to you."

Amos gave sort of a sad, manly sigh, but Clair forged ahead with her mission. "By the way, how's the case going? Closing in on the murderer yet?"

Amos recovered with the new subject. "We're working Farlow's strategy, sorting through the obvious suspects."

Anita leaned in. "Who do you think did it?"

His eyes widened and he glanced over his shoulder. I wondered if Farlow had told him to keep quiet about their suspicions. "Too soon to tell. You've got to understand, there are a slew of suspects in this case. Farlow's got a whole list."

Anita tilted her head and took a minute. "That many? I can't think of anyone who would be able to murder the man. We were thinking it must be someone from out of town, since Mr. Gold wasn't local."

Amos took a long drink of coffee and blotted his

mouth with the napkin. "It's true we don't know if he was acquainted with anyone from Evelynton. Only Ms. Lane, who admitted she contacted him to request his presence at the festival."

Clair shook her head rather vigorously. "I never met the man. Found his blog on the Internet and emailed him."

Officer Smith leaned back and gazed at the ceiling. "So you said in your statement. In these cases, we begin with known suspects. The most obvious, of course, is Melanie D'agostino."

Anita lurched forward and almost fell out of her chair. "No! She's a child."

"Eighteen. And let's not forget, she's the granddaughter of a convicted murderer."

"That's true, but you can't blame Melanie for her grandmother's mental illness."

"Her uncle was in on it, too. Sometimes that sort of thing runs in families. Farlow says they never proved conclusively that the girl wasn't involved. He thinks the judge let her go because he had a soft spot for young girls. His daughter was about the same age."

Amos shrugged. "When you think about it, Farlow has a point. It might not be a coincidence she happened to find the body. First on the scene. Did she arrange that because she knew about the corpse? Who would suspect her if she raised the alert?"

I'd been listening to the exchange and couldn't keep quiet any longer. "I'll never believe Melanie did it. She couldn't help getting caught up in that other thing with her grandmother."

I noticed my cup was getting low and thought about going for a refill, but I might miss something.

"How about the murder weapon? Have you found it? Do you know what was used?"

"Haven't found anything, but we're still working on it. It's only a matter of time."

Anita had pulled a notebook from her purse and was taking notes. "You said there were lots of suspects. Who else is on the list?"

Amos scratched his ear, glanced over his shoulder and whispered. "The next one that comes to mind is Ava Kraus. I suppose you heard she had met the victim?"

This caught Clair mid-sip and she spit coffee on the table. "No way! Why is Farlow still harping on her? She had a perfectly good explanation."

Amos used a napkin to blot the coffee drops. "The evidence speaks for itself. The body turned up right outside this place. It's the only business to use that particular dumpster. That's the physical evidence."

Amos shifted in his seat. "We're all aware Ava was entered in the festival contest that Gold happened to be judge of. Maybe she already knew he was against her. Then of course there's the fact that she changed her original story."

"I can't sit still and listen to this." Anita stood and turned her back to us, to gaze out the window. The glass steamed up as she spoke. "Those so-called facts don't mean anything. Lots of businesses here in town were taking part in the contest. Besides, a trophy in the shape of a silver marshmallow wouldn't be worth killing someone."

"People have killed for less."

Clair eyed Amos. "You sound like a television detective."

Amos's cheeks grew pink. "I've always wanted to use that line."

He paused and focused on his cup for a moment. Glancing at me, he said, "The next person on Farlow's list is you, Ms. Halloren."

I dropped my cinnamon roll and had to fish it out of my coffee mug. "Why me? What reason would he have? I mean besides the fact that he's been trying to arrest me since I moved back to town four years ago?"

Amos sighed. "I didn't want to believe him, but Jimmy explained there have only been three suspicious deaths, now four, in Evelynton, in the last fifty years. They've all occurred since you arrived." Amos stared into my eyes. Was he waiting to see my reaction?

I sputtered, suddenly not feeling so safe with this gentle man. "That doesn't mean a thing. I can't help it if bodies drop near me. And you make it sound like I'm a stranger who just showed up. I left after high school and have returned home."

Anita turned away from the window to face us. "You know, Amos, Lauren wasn't the only one at those other crime scenes. Clair was with her when they found two of the bodies."

Clair slopped coffee as she pivoted in her chair and reached out to slap Anita's shoulder. "Hey! Nice way to throw me under the bus. You want him to put me on the suspect list?"

Amos laughed. "Sorry to say you're on the list too, but a little farther down."

Clair's forehead crinkled as she mopped up the spilled coffee. The table was going to need scrubbing. "Who else are you looking at?"

Amos went on. "There's Konrad Kraus." He put up

a hand. "Before you tell me he's a great guy, I already know that. He's on my bowling team. But being Ava's husband puts him under suspicion."

Amos put up the other hand to ward off the coming protests. "We know how protective Konrad is of Ava. What if he believed Gold had romantic designs? He's a muscular guy, and had easy access to the dumpster."

Amos glanced at the door and downed the last dregs of his coffee. "It's been nice talking to you ladies, but I better get back to the station. Thanks for letting me sit with you."

The policeman ambled out to the sidewalk, and I put my elbows on the table to prop up my head. "Ugh. That was depressing. Why is Farlow considering me? I wasn't even here when Melanie found the body."

Clair glanced at me. "That's right. You were late to our meeting. Where were you?"

"What do you mean, where was I? Crawling out of bed. You know very well I have a hard time getting to early meetings. I'm insulted."

"Sorry. I know you didn't have anything to do with this. Guess I got spooked when my friend tagged me as a suspect." She cut her eyes to Anita. "I noticed he didn't mention your name."

No one ever suspected Anita of anything bad. Even in high school when Clair and I would get into trouble, everyone thought of Anita as innocent.

Anita slid into her chair, innocent blue eyes sparkling. "I'm sure I'm in there someplace. Amos didn't get to the whole list."

I had a suspicion Anita was jealous that Clair and I were suspects and she wasn't.

Anita continued. "This death has everyone on edge.

I've said it before. We should get the Woman's Detective Agency back together and solve it ourselves."

Clair and I swung toward our enthusiastic friend. In unison, we said, "No!"

I locked eyes with Anita. "We never formed a Woman's Detective Agency. It's something you made up."

"Okay. I did, but I still think it's a good idea." Anita sat silently for a minute. "We can't let Farlow blame poor Melanie D'agostino. She's just now getting over her grandmother and uncle being in jail."

Clair leaned back in her chair. "I don't suspect Melanie, but none of the other people Amos mentioned could have done it either. We know them. They aren't killers."

Anita's blond curls flew as she shook her head. "This is wrong. If Farlow focuses on the suspects Amos mentioned, and no one else, someone will be wrongfully accused. He'll never apprehend the real killer."

Clair tapped a well-manicured fingernail on the table. "Maybe we could supply alternative suspects."

I was reluctant, but had to ask. "How would we do that?"

Anita held up her notebook. "Like I said, the Woman's Detective Agency"

"No." I shut my eyes. When I opened them, Clair was staring at me. I'd obviously lost her support.

Clair turned to Anita. "Just until we come up with another list of suspects to give Farlow. He'll need help in this. We all know he isn't particularly creative."

I couldn't argue the logic. "Okay. We'll work on alternatives, suggest them to Farlow, and then we stop.

Agreed?"

"Agreed." Clair nodded decisively.

"Let's each think about it tonight, and meet tomorrow with our lists." Anita's reaction was almost gleeful at the prospect. You'd have thought I'd suggested a trip to the amusement park instead of a journey into a murder's mind.

Would I live to regret reviving the Woman's Detective Agency?

Chapter Eight

Burgers 'N Bean Sprouts, on the outskirts of town, was a vintage-themed burger joint fashioned from what had once been a filling station. The place had lots of atmosphere and pretty good food, if an odd assortment of trendy toppings. It seemed like a good spot for the first meeting of the Woman's Detective Agency.

Anita laid down the two page menu. "It's beyond me why anyone would put bean sprouts on a good hamburger. I love to cook, and I'm willing to try all kinds of sauces and such, but I draw the line at sprouts." She smiled at the young waitress dressed in a poodle skirt and sweater. "I'll take tomato, onion, provolone cheese, and romaine on mine."

Clair placed her board on top of Anita's. "You can load my burger with sprouts. Oh, and I'll take sweet potato fries. They're the best." She flashed her newly whitened teeth at us. "Girls, we're in our forties." As if I could forget. "We must take every opportunity to make our meals vitamin rich."

I added my menu to the stack. "The Country

Burger, please, with ketchup, mayonnaise, and mustard. Definitely no sprouts. But I'll agree with Clair on the sweet potato fries." In truth, I didn't understand how anything deep fried and tasting like dessert could claim health benefits.

The waitress made her way to the kitchen and Anita pulled out her notebook. "Let's get right to the meeting. Where are your suspect lists?"

Crap. I was hoping we would eat first, giving me time to think. I feigned a need to tie my shoe and dropped beneath the table. Then untied it and tied it again. My plan was to hide just out of Anita's line of vision and listen to Clair's thoughts. Maybe she would give me the prompt I needed. Then, if I scribbled fast enough they wouldn't suspect I'd failed in the homework assignment.

I continued the ruse until things had gone quiet up above. Was my absence noticed? I peeked over the edge of the table. Anita drummed her fingers and stared at Clair.

My Realtor friend held a brand new notepad, still wrapped in cellophane. She whined. "I was swamped with work last night. I really did consider it, in the limited time I had." She dropped the pristine notebook on the table. "Couldn't think of anyone."

Anita turned her attention to me, still under the table, fiddling with my shoelace. It was getting embarrassing. How many minutes does it take to tie a shoe?

The truth would have to be told. I pulled myself up into the chair and blurted out my defense. "I made an attempt. Spent time thinking about it, even asked Mason. But we didn't come up with any names, either."

I held up my empty notebook.

Anita blew out a breath and gazed at the ceiling. "I'm disappointed. I thought you ladies would have loads of ideas."

Oh, the shame of failure. "I'm sorry, and will try to be of more help in the future. We need a jump-start. Let's talk about your suspects."

Anita's eyes widened and she clutched her steno pad to her chest.

I waited expectantly, and glanced at Clair.

A lopsided smile crossed Clair's face. "No names on your list?"

Anita slumped. "No. Couldn't think of even one. I guess, as investigators, we're all out of practice."

Fortunately, our waitress arrived with lunch, giving us something positive to consider. We spent the next few minutes in conversation of little consequence other than the quality of the burgers and the freshness of the bread.

I finished my sandwich and took my time with the fries. Dabbing my lips with a napkin, I decided it was up to me to get things underway. "Okay, let's think about everyone who could have committed the crime."

Anita nodded and pulled out her pen.

Clair, whose mind had wandered, arranged her half-eaten burger on her plate. "Look how artfully the sprouts spilled out around my sandwich. That will make a great picture." She handed me her phone. "Take of shot of me, so I can post it on my site."

I obligingly snapped a few shots of Clair posing as food model. "Now. Let's talk business."

Before anyone could begin, the chef strode out of the kitchen, heading to our table. "You must love my creations if you're taking pictures of it. Was it everything you wished for?"

Clair gushed dramatically. "Carl, the cuisine is superb. I can't tell you how thrilled I am to have healthy alternatives for lunch."

"I do my best to offer top quality ingredients and great flavor, at a reasonable price. Did you know Burgers 'N Bean Sprouts is entered in the festival this year? I was keeping it a secret but everyone will know soon enough. I've been working all year on—you won't believe this—a healthy marshmallow. It's all vegetable, and sweetened with herbs."

Clair tipped her head and squinted her eyes. "Oh. That's interesting."

I couldn't muster up more than a blank stare, as I pictured a green, leafy marshmallow.

Anita's expression saved Carl's ego. She glowed, her eyes sparkled, and she chirped, "How exciting! Can we try one?"

"No, couldn't do that. Keeping it a well-guarded secret. After I win the grand prize, the Sprout Mallow will be available with every meal. "Too bad the big shot food critic got killed, but I think the mayor will do a fine job. I talked to him today, when he came to pick up lunch. Told him he should have been the judge in the first place. Can't imagine what imbecile chose a stranger to pass judgment on Evelynton's food."

As chairman of the festival committee, Clair kept her righteous indignation to herself and stuffed another bite of her sandwich into her mouth.

"I'll get back to my kitchen. You ladies have a good day." Carl sauntered toward the kitchen.

Anita snagged one of Clair's fries. "I'm glad to see

Carl's excited about the festival. He's been grumpy other years, because he says Ava always wins. I remember four years ago he even complained in the newspaper that anyone who put their customer's well-being ahead of profits didn't have a chance in the contest. Said all anyone needed to do, in this town, was pour on the sugar to win a prize."

I laughed and accidently spit out a piece of sweet potato fry. "It's the Marshmallow Festival, for goodness sake. Of course there's sugar."

Clair scooped a few more fries onto Anita's plate. "We've needed the festival to come back. We lost a big source of revenue when the old marshmallow factory burned down. Carl should have helped to support the festival, and been happy."

Her brow creased. After a moment, she grabbed her notebook and tore at the wrapping. "I have my first suspect. And he just walked into the kitchen of Burgers 'N Bean Sprouts. Hand me a pen."

Why hadn't I thought of Carl? "You're right. He's spent years building up resentment over the outcome of the contest. What if he got rid of Giles Gold so his friend the mayor would be called in as a replacement?" I pulled out a pencil and printed Carl Rocco on the first line of my notepad.

With new enthusiasm, we gathered our belongings and marched to the counter to pay our tabs.

When Anita had paid, she pivoted toward us sporting a gleeful smile. Her favorite game had begun. She whispered, "The first thing to find out is where Carl was on the night of the murder. I'll talk to the waitress. Bet she knows his schedule."

My blond friend sidled up to the teen as Clair and I

retreated to the parking lot. A few minutes later she scooted out the door.

"Margo, that's the waitress, told me her boss worked late Tuesday night and was in early Wednesday morning. She was certain because he always works the same schedule."

Anita scribbled in her notebook. "I also found out he's married, and I don't recall seeing his wife's name on any of my committees. It's my civic duty to visit her."

Clair had come up with a suspect. Anita was racing into the investigation. I was being left behind. I don't know how long I sat in my car after my friends drove away. I needed to remember why people called me a detective.

After sorting through all I knew about the case, a thought rose to the surface. We didn't know, yet, why Giles Gold had arrived in town weeks before he was expected. How long had he been here? Did he spend the night? If he had, he must have talked to someone.

And I intended to find that someone.

Chapter Nine

My mission, for the day, was to check out lodging in Evelynton. I figured this wouldn't be much of a problem. There were only two motels, no hotels, and one bed and breakfast. I would go first to the motels. They were close. The B and B sat a few miles outside the town, near the interstate. How any of the establishments stayed in business was a mystery since Evelynton wasn't what anyone would call a destination city.

Anne's Stay Inn was located about a mile from Burgers 'N Bean Sprouts, so I went there first. The office looked like a little Swiss cottage, with shutters on the windows and flower boxes underneath, sprouting weathered artificial flowers. Evelynton does not have a Swiss heritage, but the motel was cute in an old-fashioned sort of way. I'd heard the rooms hadn't been updated since the eighties, but were kept clean. That from the motel's cleaning lady, Gladys, who also cleaned the Rare Curl.

There were a few cars in the lot. I took a space by the entrance marked Office. As soon as I opened the

Chrysler door I was treated to blaring music and shrieking of what I recognized as a TV game show. Not my favorite sound.

I steeled myself and walked into the building. The man at the desk ignored me, his attention centered on a small television hanging on the wall. The chair, he sat in, tipped back on its back legs while his feet rested on the counter. I hesitated to disturb him. He could have easily lost control of his precarious seating arrangement.

I shuffled my feet and cleared my throat until I gained his attention. He wrestled the chair into a stable position and jumped up to turn down the TV volume.

I introduced myself and asked if he remembered a guest named Giles Gold. He said he didn't.

I showed him a picture I'd printed from the Internet, pulled from Gold's blog. It was grainy. My printer isn't the best. The clerk didn't recognize him, but said there was another person who worked at the desk occasionally. I could ask the other guy but he wouldn't be in until the weekend.

I'd envisioned my investigation being a bit more fruitful. So far, my time had been useless. Before I left the parking lot, I looked up the address of the other motel.

Wallowing in self-pity, I drove past the E-Town Gardens entrance before I noticed the sign. The building was set back off the road and of a simple, stream-lined design. It was not new by any means, and I didn't see any gardens, but I thought the modern architecture might have been more appealing to the New York native. I executed a U-turn and drove into the parking lot. There were plenty of empty parking places, as I'd expected.

A woman at the desk showed some interest when I walked in. I introduced myself, and asked if anyone by the name of Giles Gold had been registered there.

She assured me that no one by that name had ever stayed E-Town Gardens, and asked how many nights I'd like to book.

"I'm not interested in renting a room here." A shadow passed over her eyes, so I attempted to redeem myself. "But only because I live in town and have no need of accommodations. Otherwise, this would definitely be my choice of lodging."

The clerk maintained eye contact, but the smile had begun to slide from her face. I pushed ahead. "It's possible that Mr. Gold used another name. I have a picture." I pulled out the photo.

The woman took the photo and held it close to her eyes. "No. Haven't seen him. How about a one- or two-night getaway package? We often rent to towns people looking for a weekend retreat."

"Do you have a pool?"

"No. We have a game room."

"I'll keep that in mind."

I thanked the woman, retrieved the photo, and returned it to my bag. Leaving the office, I almost ran into a man entering as I was going out. Before the door closed behind him, I heard "Thanks for filling in, June. I'll take over."

With a tinge of giddiness at another opportunity, I stepped back inside, and stuck out my hand. "Hi. My name is Lauren Halloren."

He gave me a look that I would use before saying, "I don't want any," but shook my hand and introduced himself as Frank.

I charged ahead. "I was just asking June about someone who might have stayed here. Do you happen to remember the name Giles Gold?"

"Sure, that's the fella they found in the dumpster. Everyone's talking about it."

"Yes. That's the one. Is it possible he spent the night here?"

"Not a chance. No one called Giles ever stayed here. I see all the names on the book. That's one I'd remember, and I try to meet all our guests. Like to keep track of the activity in the place."

"It's possible he used a different name, since he was famous. Might have wanted to stay incognito. Here's his picture."

I pulled the now rumpled photo from my bag, and smoothed out the wrinkles on the desk.

"That's Giles Gold?"

"That's him. The picture is from his Internet blog so I don't know how recent it is."

"Well, isn't that something. He stayed here a couple nights. Said his name was Bob Smith and he looked like a regular guy, but that's him."

Frank took the photo and showed it to June. "Look at that. We had a celebrity right here at E-Town Gardens."

Returning his attention to me, he said, "He paid cash in advance for three nights. Said he might stay longer and would pay me when he decided. I was surprised to see he'd checked out after only two days. Cleared out early in the morning, and left his key in the mail slot."

"I wonder if you would show me the room he

stayed in?"

"Sure. But I'll warn you it's nothing special, just like all the other rooms. And if you're looking for souvenirs, you won't find any. The maid's cleaned it by now. We pride ourselves in clean rooms and they get done as soon as a guest vacates it. I want it prepared for the next guest."

I followed Frank down the row of rooms. He stopped at room number four-ten and unlocked the door.

I don't know why I expected this to be exciting. The room was neat and tidy, and looked exactly like a motel room. One double bed, one nightstand, uninteresting framed cardboard print on the wall. An old model television sitting on an even older dresser. I checked out the bathroom. That didn't take long since it was small with no crooks or crannies someone might store anything. The lights were bright and illuminated every crevice.

On TV, they always find a clue, maybe a cigarette butt or a matchbook. I searched everywhere, and went over it a second time. There was nothing in this room.

The only place I hadn't checked was under the bed. I looked at the carpet. It had been swept, but it sure wasn't anything I'd want to crawl around on. Who knew when it had been shampooed? In any case, in the interest of being thorough, I sucked in a breath, got down on my knees and took a look, only to learn the bed sat on a platform. Not to appear surprised by this, I examined the floor around it. Nothing, except enough dust to prove the maid hadn't used the crevice attachment.

I'd almost gotten up when I noticed a glint of shine

at the edge of the platform. I moved close to the floor, keeping my face away from the rug, and reached for it. An earring, a gold toned leaf covered with blue and green rhinestones. Larger and flashier than I would ever want, though Clair might wear something like it when she got dressed up. I was pretty sure the bangle didn't belong to Giles Gold. It most likely had been lost by some tenant visiting the establishment months previously. Even so, I slid the earring into my pocket.

I thanked Frank, and left the room, feeling deflated and remembering why I chose not to be a detective. The man bid me goodbye and began to stride toward the office.

"Hey Frank," came a shout from the other end of the walkway. "I thought you were getting me a new wash cart."

Frank pivoted and shouted back to a young woman pulling a cart loaded with cleaning supplies. "I did. They were supposed to have delivered it. Are you sure it isn't sitting back at the utility closet? Go look again. I told 'em to leave it there."

"If I'd found a decent wash cart, do you think I'd be pushing this old thing? The squawking's about to make me go deaf."

She gave the cart a jerk. "If you don't believe me, go look for yourself."

"Don't get riled, Cheryl. I believe you. I'll call the company and see what's going on." Frank turned and hurried to the office.

Seizing the opportunity to extend my investigation, I walked toward the maid, who had continued her noisy trek toward me. Cheryl was right. The closer I got, the more obnoxious the sound of her wash cart. "Hi Cheryl,

I wonder if you'd mind answering a question."

The woman checked her watch and pulled a stick of gum from her pocket. "I've got a minute. What do you want to know?"

"I'm asking around to see if Giles Gold stayed at this motel." Once more, I pulled out the picture. "Frank said he recognized him but he'd used an assumed name."

Cheryl's eyes softened. "Oh, I remember him. He was nice." She twinkled when she described him as older, but a cutie.

"We talked for quite a while." She glanced toward the office where her boss could be seen in his desk chair. "Probably longer than Frank would approve of, but he wants us to be nice to the customers."

"His name wasn't Giles. I'd remember that. I think he said it was Bob. He asked me for advice."

Cheryl chuckled. "It isn't often a guest wants to talk to me, the maid, let alone ask my opinion."

"He said he had a crush on a woman in town, so he flew in from New York to surprise her. Imagine a man traveling all the way here from New York, just to show her he loved her. Isn't that romantic?"

I was impressed. I hadn't been on the receiving end of that kind of attention for a long time. "That was certainly romantic. What kind of advice did he need?"

"He wanted to know how to make the best impression when he saw her. I told him the best thing he could do was to take flowers. No woman could resist him if he showed up with a bouquet. And he had to get the flowers from George and Larry's Florist on Main Street. He wasn't to stop at a filling station or grocery store."

"Good advice. Who was the lucky lady?"

"Wouldn't tell me her name. He asked me for a phone book so he could look up her address. Took me a while to find one. Who uses phone books anymore?"

"I thought it was funny he didn't know her address. Must not have known her very well. When I think about it, that's even more romantic."

"Was he successful with the woman?"

"I don't know. He checked out. I got the impression he might stay a few days, and even thought he'd make a point of telling me how he got along with his girlfriend. But the next day, Frank called me to clean the room. Bob didn't even stick around long enough to let me know what happened with his lady friend. Maybe the woman of his dreams broke his heart. I hope he finds someone else."

"When you went in to clean, did you find anything? Had he left anything behind?"

"Nothing unusual. It was just the regular room cleaning." After a moment, Cheryl shook her head. "There was one funny thing."

She stepped closer, and whispered. "A blanket was missing from the room. I never would have pegged him for someone who would steal. Silly thing to take. It was old, threadbare. It wasn't worth anything, so I didn't tell Frank. I just got a replacement from the cupboard."

She shifted her gaze down the walk to the office. "I protected him, even though he didn't think enough of me to stick around long enough to let me know what happened."

The maid hefted a mop from the cart. "Guess I'd better get to work."

Cheryl let herself into one of the rooms. I wasn't

going to be the one to tell her that her friend, Bob, was
dead.

Chapter Ten

How many scoops for a carafe of coffee? It had been a while since I brewed a whole pot at home. I added ground coffee. Three heaping spoonfuls. Crap. That didn't look right. I threw in another and punched the start button. Better too strong than wimpy. Soon the aroma of brewed coffee drifted through the house. If I closed my eyes, I could imagine I was in Ava's Java.

At Clair's insistence, the Woman's Detective Agency had moved our meeting place to my house. So many of our friends at the Java were actually suspects in the death of Giles Gold. Our investigation needed to be kept secret.

Mason trotted to the front door and sat down to stare at it, so I prepared to receive guests. Scarcely a minute later, I heard Anita's singsong voice and Clair's laugh on the porch. I nudged the cat with my toe, moving him aside to provide room for the door to swing open. He was incredibly useful when it came to foretelling the future, but not so aware of personal space.

Clair reached down to scratch Mason's ear and sauntered to the sofa to make herself comfortable. Mason followed and curled up on her lap. About a year earlier, Clair had decided to be an animal person, and no longer worried about cat hair on her designer suits.

Anita dove into the subject of the day, as she hoofed it to the kitchen. "If Carl, from Burgers 'N Bean Sprouts, could be a suspect, we also have to consider Ava and her husband. Everyone who was at the Java that day, or the day before, is a possibility.

She grabbed the carafe and filled three mugs. "For that matter, one of us could have done it. No playing favorites."

I carried two cups to the living room. "Let's not get paranoid. We know none of us is homicidal."

Once I'd served Clair and taken a chair, she held her notebook above the sleeping cat. "Let's get started. My first suspect is Carl Rocco. His motive? The burning desire to win the marshmallow competition. More importantly, he confessed to wanting his pal the mayor to be the celebrity judge. That position was conveniently vacated with the death of Giles Gold."

Anita put her coffee cup on the end table and studied her notes. "I checked on Rocco's window of opportunity, but I'm not clear on it. The waitress said he was working at the time we think Gold was killed, but she didn't actually see him, so how do we know?"

Anita put a check mark on her notes and continued. "I went to Carl's home on the ruse of asking his wife to be part of the church rummage sale. She said no. Probably thought I was crazy since we'd never met, but we had a nice conversation.

She told me Carl arrived home late on the day of

the murder. That would be the day before Gold's body was found. She said there was nothing odd about the late arrival. He'd been working a lot of hours, getting ready for the festival."

I cleared my throat. "I have new information. It might change the direction of our investigation."

My friends turned expectant eyes to me, and I related the details of my visit to E-Town Gardens.

Anita's eyes got big and she shrieked. "Giles Gold had a girlfriend? That is exciting. It opens up all sorts of possibilities."

Clair didn't shriek, but close to it. "Why didn't you tell us this as soon as we got here? It changes everything."

The ruckus woke Mason and prompted a dramatic leap from Clair's lap. He galloped to the dining room and crouched under the table. The sudden departure caused Clair to drop her notebook.

Anita cut her gaze to me. "Now we're getting somewhere. Who is she?"

I blew out a breath. "Sorry, I don't know. Still working on that."

"Oh. At least it's a lead." Clair retrieved her notebook. "Another woman. That's interesting. I wonder if his wife know about it."

Somewhat deflated, I said, "I don't know that either. Guess my next move is contacting Mrs. Gold. But from what Cheryl, the maid, said even the girlfriend was unaware of his infatuation."

It was time to pull out my prize. "I do have something tangible." I held up the earring.

Clair snatched it from my hand. "Isn't that pretty. Where did you get it?"

"I thought you'd like it. Sort of your style isn't it?" I related the details of my search, and confessed to the doubtful origin of the jewelry. "There was a lot of dust under there, so it could have been lost weeks ago. Months?"

Anita stirred sugar into her coffee. "I bet it belongs to his girlfriend. That's proof there was a woman in his room. Maybe she killed him."

I held out my hand. "I'm going to put it in an envelope for safekeeping."

Clair handed over the bobble, shaking her head. "Ladies, let's not get too excited. This might not have anything to do with the murder. Like Lauren said, it could have been dropped by some tenant months ago."

Anita took a moment to write in her notebook. "Great work, Lauren. You can keep working on that angle. Is there any point in discussing anything else?"

Clair put up a hand. "Let's not get stuck on one lead. There are other suspects."

She waited a moment and then continued. "What do you think about Melanie D'agostino? Could she be a murderer?"

Anita stiffened. "We've discussed her involvement before. I don't think she's a killer and the girl's certainly not big enough to overpower a grown man. If she did manage to kill him, how would she move his body to the dumpster? She had to have help."

Mason crept in from the dining room and crawled into my lap. I pulled my notebook from under him. "Anita's right. No way could she have done it alone. And her criminal relatives are in jail, so I don't see how we can consider her. Besides, she's a sweet young girl."

Anita tapped her steno pad. "I confess, I already

checked with some of Melanie's friends. There's no boyfriend in the picture. I don't consider her a suspect."

Clair glanced at her friend. "You've been busy." She flipped a page of her notebook. "Next suspect— Ava. I won't believe she did it. She's not capable of murder. But what about Konrad? None of us know him well. He's big enough, and would have had motive if he was protecting Ava." After a moment, she raised her pen. "And opportunity."

Anita leaned forward. "What if Ava was the girlfriend? Konrad could have found out, and been jealous."

Clair added. "Or Giles might have made a pass at her? Maybe got aggressive. I imagine Konrad could be violent."

I felt like sinking into my chair, but needed to add my thoughts. "What if Ava rebuffed Giles? He could even have threatened to ruin the Java's reputation on his blog."

I lifted Mason into a hug. "Crap. Everything seems to point to Ava or Konrad, or both."

Anita shook her steno pad. "We aren't helping. Nothing in our investigation is apt to divert Farlow's attention from his prime suspects."

Clair gazed at me. "In fact, we're making everything worse. One of our friends is going to go to jail."

Chapter Eleven

I heeded the call for another meeting of the Woman's Detective Agency right after my shift at The Rare Curl. This time we met at Ava's Java. As soon as I joined my fellow sleuths, Anita planted her elbows on the table and locked eyes with me. "So, tell us what you've discovered about the earring."

Clair leaned in next to her and whispered. "Does it belong to Ava?"

I stared back at them. "How would I know? I've only had it a day, and I worked at the reception desk this morning."

Anita narrowed her eyes. "Oh. I thought you would have been working out the details. You know—in your brain."

Would they never give up on the idea that I'm a genius crime-fighter? "Sorry to disappoint."

Anita sat back in her chair, shaking her head. "It doesn't belong to Ava. I've been thinking about it. She would never wear such gaudy jewelry."

Clair cut her eyes to Anita. "Gaudy? I'd call it bold. And she might wear something like it when she got dressed up. Maybe if she and Konrad were to go on a date."

Anita smirked. "Not a chance. Ava has a classy, dignified vibe. I see her in understated eighteen carat gold earrings."

"Bold jewelry can be classy. Right Lauren?"

I wrapped my hands around my warm coffee mug. "Don't pull me into that discussion. I don't even wear jewelry." That would mean I'd have to dress up. And I hadn't been on a date in months.

"But getting back to the investigation, let's remember the earring might not mean anything. The important evidence is the news of the girlfriend."

Anita sighed. "You're right. We have reliable testimony of that. What's next on your agenda?"

"I'll drive back over to the motel later and ask questions. Maybe someone noticed a woman around Gold's room."

Clair nodded. "And if they saw a tall woman, we'll know it was Ava."

Anita glared at her friend. "It wasn't Ava! She'd already taken care of his advances at the food conference and would never have gone to his room."

Clair put up a hand. "Just trying to be objective." She glanced over her shoulder. "Let's keep our voices down. Remember where we are."

We sat at our favorite table at Ava's Java. Small round, plenty of room for three, next to the window. It had been our spot since I'd joined my friends, four years earlier.

Anita ducked her chin and whispered. "We should have chosen another location for our meeting. Maybe at Lauren's again."

Clair shook her head. "We can't do that. We always meet here. Ava would suspect something if we didn't show up."

"You're right. I wouldn't want her to think we're avoiding her. We'll just have to be careful." Anita sat back, looking innocent while whispering. "Have you told Farlow about your discovery of the girlfriend?"

I put up a hand. "No, and I won't. First of all, Officer Farlow would never believe me. I'll wait until I have a name. He knows Gold flirted with Ava at the food conference. We don't want to supply another reason for him to suspect her." I leaned back and pulled my coffee close. "I'll let the police department do their own investigation. They're the professionals."

"It seems dishonest to withhold information. I think you should tell them."

"Do you know how many times Farlow's told me to stay out of police business?"

Anita's blond curls bounced as she shook her head. "Lost count."

"Someday he'll find a reason to put me in jail. I won't talk to him unless I have solid evidence."

Anita continued. "I know how we can prove Ava's innocence." When both Clair and I gave her our full attention, she said, "What if we drop the earring on the floor for Ava to find? If she claims it, we'll know she was in the hotel room. If she doesn't, we'll know she's not the girlfriend."

I shook my head. "We don't even know it belongs to the girlfriend."

Anita shrugged. "True. But it's a start."

Clair pointed an index finger at Anita. "If the earring isn't hers, she'll put it at the counter to find the owner."

"Perfect! Then when someone claims it, we'll have our suspect."

"That's actually a good idea." I pulled the envelope, holding the earring, from my bag.

We all jumped at Ava's voice. She stood next to us holding the coffee carafe. "What are you girls whispering about? Must be some good gossip and I need a distraction. What is it?"

We stared up at Ava with wide eyes. I slid the envelope into a pocket and put my other hand to my throat. I whispered-hoarsely. "Unfortunately not gossip. I have laryngitis. Woke up with it. Been getting worse all day."

"Oh no. It must have been difficult answering the phone at Rarity's." Ava's concern pinged my guilt at the lie.

Anita bobbed her head. "Isn't it silly? Lauren can't help but speak like that. Clair and I just end up whispering too." She gave a short, sort of hysterical, hiccup of laughter.

Ava's eyebrows drew together as she refilled our cups. "I hope you feel better soon, Lauren. Why don't I get you some tea and honey?"

I croaked. "Oh, no. I have throat lozenges. But, thank you."

"Take care of yourself and get some rest." Ava stepped away.

As the barista mingled with her other customers, Clair glared at me. "What kind of excuse was that? I bet she didn't believe a word of it."

"It's the first thing that came to mind. I'm a terrible liar."

Clair closed her eyes and shook her head. "And Anita, you didn't help any."

Anita stifled a nervous giggle. "Sorry. Got caught off guard."

I gasped as Anita snatched the envelope from my pocket, pulled out the earring and tossed it under a neighboring table.

I stared at her, speechless.

Watching the bobble slide across the floor, Clair took a deep breath. "Okay, I guess that's taken care of. Let's work on other areas of the investigation." She shifted her gaze to the coffee counter and whispered. "No mention of Ava or Konrad."

Anita nodded. "Good idea."

After taking a moment to come to terms with the theft, I mouthed, "Let's discuss alternative suspects."

My friends leaned in. "What?"

I pointed at my throat, and mouthed the words again.

"Very funny." Clair leaned back in her chair.

"Oh, I got it. I know what she said." Anita whispered. "Alternative suspects."

Clair sighed and flipped to a new page of her notebook. "Gold had thousands of readers. He could have made any number of enemies from a review of a restaurant they liked, or didn't like, or by giving a bad rating to their own establishment."

I hissed. "Maybe someplace here in Evelynton, or nearby."

Clair tapped the table with a newly manicured nail. "Did he ever write a negative review of a place in or near Evelynton? If he did, I missed it."

Anita waved off the question. "I'm one of his faithful readers. Love his blog. He posts so many great cooking ideas. But he never mentioned any place here in town. I'd remember." She added sugar to her coffee. "Too bad there won't be any new content."

Clair kept tapping the table with her polished red nails. "We didn't even know he was in town. How would someone else know?"

Anita looked to me for a comment. I pointed to my throat and mouthed. "Don't want to strain my voice."

My friends narrowed their eyes at me.

Anita sipped her coffee. "What about family members?"

I widened my eyes, smiled, and pointed at her.

Clair glanced at Anita. "They say it's usually the spouse or someone close to the victim."

I nodded vigorously.

I was enjoying the charade, although I think my friends were tiring of my humor.

We were startled once again when Ava hurried to our table, a twisted a dish towel in her hands. "Guess what. Beverly, from B's Bed and Breakfast, just picked up an order and wanted to let me know. The Gold family is coming back to town. They just booked a reservation with her for the three days of the festival."

Wringing the towel tighter, "I know I shouldn't be nervous, but he was found right outside. It's like a nightmare that won't end."

Clair put a hand on Ava's arm. "Don't worry. Everyone agrees it was an unfortunate coincidence. We know you had nothing to do with the murder."

"Such good friends. Thank you." The barista pivoted to return to work but stopped short. She crouched and retrieved the earring, shoving it into the pocket of her apron before scurrying to the counter.

Chapter Twelve

A nita and I can usually comment on everything. But the moment our eyes met we were both stunned into silence. Anita's head tipped to the side, reminding me of Mason when eyeing a fly trapped behind a window screen.

I waited for a comment from Clair, but she silently gazed after Ava, seemingly equally fascinated.

Someone had to break the trance. Hefting my handbag to my shoulder, I collected my notebook. "We can't keep standing here. Get your things. Let's continue our conversation outside." The three of us shoved our chairs under the table and shuffled to the door, where I took a last longing glance at the shop keeper.

"Wait. Look."

Clair and Anita skidded to a halt at the open door and stared at me. Trying not to attract attention, I motioned with my eyes, and whispered. "Look beside the cash register."

Anita followed my instructions and slapped herself on the chest. "There's the earring. It wasn't Ava's after all. She set it out for someone to claim." She grabbed Clair's arm. "Such a relief. I knew Ava had nothing to do with the man's death."

Clair finally turned her eyes to the coffee counter. "Hmm. You're right. It appears the earring belongs to someone else. And I'm glad of that, but it doesn't automatically exonerate Ava."

Anita used her grip on Clair's arm to guide her outside. "Clair Lane, I don't know how you can even consider it."

Clair shrugged. "I agree Ava doesn't seem like the type to kill anyone. I said that to keep us objective." After a glance at her watch, she continued. "Got to get back to work. Appointments this afternoon. Talk to you ladies, later." She darted across the street, defying oncoming traffic.

Belatedly, I shouted. "Be careful, you'll get hit." But Clair had reached the sidewalk and walked on without response.

Anita pulled her keys from her purse. "What's with her?"

"Probably stress. It's getting to all of us. Detective work is no fun if you suspect a friend of murder." Traffic cleared and we proceeded to the parking lot. "I'll drive over to the motel and ask questions. Hopefully someone saw something."

Anita tailed me to my Chrysler and I twisted toward her. "Isn't that your car on the other side, by the Toyota?"

Replacing her keys in her handbag, she nodded. "A thought just hit me. The two of us work better as a team. I'll go with you. While you question the manager, I'll canvas the property for possible witnesses." She was right. Anita had a gift for getting people to talk. I didn't.

My gregarious friend sat in the passenger seat with pen poised over her notebook. "What questions do you think I should ask?"

"You're assuming there will be someone to question."

"Don't be discouraging. Think positively. I'm counting on being in the right place to meet the right person."

"Huh." I guessed that was as good a plan as any.

When we arrived, Frank was perched in front of the TV. I guess televisions are a necessity to relieve boredom in small town motels. He didn't show any signs of recognizing me, so I introduced myself and reminded him of the famous person who had stayed in his establishment.

The light appeared in his eyes, and I began my interrogation. The questioning didn't go well. He hadn't noticed anyone suspicious in the area, even though he was adamant that he kept a watchful an eye on the property. I concluded he mainly kept eyes on his TV programs. I could tell this by watching said eyes repeatedly dart back to the game show blaring on his television.

Running out of pertinent questions, and lacking game show answers, I left the office in search of Anita.

I wandered the halls for a few minutes and found her talking to a man in a green work uniform. They seemed to be in deep conversation. This was Anita's enviable gift. The knack for deep conversation with complete strangers. I trotted to them, hoping to overhear a tidbit of useful information. When I'd attracted their attention, Anita introduced me to Bud, the plumber.

Anita beamed. "Bud was telling me about some repair work he's been doing here at the motel. Almost every day for a couple of weeks."

Bud nodded. "It's been steady work. In a facility this age, when one pipe goes, they all go."

My friend's sparkling blue eyes smiled at me. "I was about to ask Bud if he'd noticed anyone hanging around room four-ten." She turned to Bud. "I'm thinking there might have been someone who didn't seem to be a registered guest."

Bud guffawed. "Lady, I can't even remember what I had for breakfast this morning."

Anita put on her compassionate face. To be fair, it wasn't an act, she was serious when she spoke to anyone. "I understand you are so busy, with taking care of all these pipes. Can't imagine how you keep everything running smoothly. But for me, would you think back? It would have been a day or so before you heard of the body discovered at Ava's Java. Think about that and maybe it will jog your memory. I bet you notice everything and don't even realize it. Maybe there was someone you passed, who caught your attention."

Bud directed his eyes to the ceiling, one hand on his chin. "Well, now that you ask, I did see a woman along this hall somewhere. I noticed her, but didn't pay much attention. Not my taste, if you know what I mean. Not enough padding on her backside. Hair too short. I like 'em a bit more womanly." Bud gave me a once over.

I scooted back a step. "What else do you remember about the woman?"

He shrugged and stuck his hands in his pockets. "Nothing. Just what I told you."

Anita attempted to pry loose more memories, but we were soon convinced Bud didn't have more to tell us.

My friend grinned at the plumber, whose eyes now scanned her for womanliness. "You have been very helpful. Thank you so much for your time."

I took Anita's arm and gently propelled her back the way we came. "Thanks, Bud. Bye." I speed-walked to the parking lot, dragging Anita with me. We jumped into the station wagon and I steered toward town. Notebook in hand, Anita recorded the description of the woman who might, or might not, have met with Giles Gold.

Cruising past the city limit sign, Melanie D'agostino stood at a crosswalk. I'd noticed her too late to wave, but watched her in the rear-view. She wasn't alone. Why hadn't I seen the man also waiting to cross? I wish I'd gotten a closer look at him. Could he be an accomplice in the murder of Giles Gold?

"Anita."

"Hmm?" She kept her head down, still scribbling in her notebook.

Curse my suspicious nature. The man might have not even been with Melanie. Could have been just another pedestrian. "Nothing."

The girl hadn't been back to work at the Java since the gruesome discovery. But who could blame her? I doubt many eighteen year old girls could put that image behind them.

Would she fit the description of 'the girlfriend'? No. At least not the description the plumber had given us. Melanie had long gorgeous locks. I'm sure he would classify that kind of hair as womanly. We couldn't be sure the woman he'd described had indeed been in Gold's room. She might have been wandering the halls for another reason.

I drove on, trying to calm frayed nerves but letting my mind wander.

How many women in Evelynton would fit Bud's description? A lot. Geesh. Even Clair fit the description. Why had I ever been interested in writing true crime? This was stressful.

After depositing Anita in the lot next to her car, I turned toward my house, but my mind still buzzed. Who did I know meeting Bud's description? Ava? She had lost weight recently. And her hair was sort of short. Was it an act when she was so casual with the earring? Did she know we were watching? We could have been more discreet.

I needed more input on the little I'd learned of the case.

I pulled out my phone and punched in a number.

Chapter Thirteen

Clair Lane had purchased her house about a year earlier, after the owner defaulted on the mortgage. Actually, the owner had passed away and lain in the house undetected for at least six months, rendering her unable to make the payments. But that's another story.

Clair opened the front door as soon as I climbed out of my car. I strode up the walkway and almost tripped over a furry creature who had run ahead of me. Looking down, I was surprised to see a black and white feline slipping through the open door. "Mason?"

Glancing at my friend, "What's my cat doing here?"

Clair chuckled. "He comes to visit me all the time. Your street isn't that far away. Did you know he only has to cut through three yards from here to be at the back of your property?"

Mason ignored me and trotted down the hallway, tail held high. I took a seat across from Clair in her living room. "He seems to be comfortable here. How did he even know where you lived?"

She shrugged. "I'm thinking about getting a kitten for him to play with while he's here."

That didn't sound like a good idea to me. "Then there will be two cats roaming the neighborhood." What if Mason decided to stay with Clair? I shook my head. No reason to accuse her of planning to steal my cat.

"But the purpose of my visit. I wanted to fill you in on what Anita and I learned at E-Town Gardens." I relayed Bud's recollection then had to add my hesitation. "It might have been his imagination. Or maybe he tried to impress Anita by supplying the information she wanted."

As I thought about the possibility of Bud inventing the unknown woman, my enthusiasm plummeted. I sank into a chair and rested my forehead in my hand. "It might have been a lie. Crap. That trip was probably a waste of time."

Clair frowned and clucked her tongue. "It does sound sketchy. But don't worry. How about we keep it in mind and continue our investigation?" Her smile returned. "I'm sure something will turn up. How about some coffee?"

"I could use a pick-me-up."

As Clair got up, Mason bounded past us on his way to the kitchen. Soon he was playing soccer with a new toy on the tile floor. "What does my cat have now? I'm so sorry. He can be such a pest, always stealing my pens to play with." I jumped up to rescue whatever he'd confiscated.

I lunged and missed the colorful ornament skidding across the floor. "He's stolen something of yours.

Always attracted to bright colors." I attempted to intercept Mason's pass and missed.

Clair was right beside me. "Don't worry. I'll get it." She crouched to reach for the toy, but Mason had long ago perfected his moves in the game of keep-away.

I was out of breath. "This is embarrassing. My cat shouldn't be taking over your house." The toy was skidding toward me. I plunged and wound up sprawled across the kitchen floor, but managed to beat both Mason and Clair to the prize.

Grasping the toy, I pulled it closer. Anita might call it gaudy. Clair would call it bold. I called it evidence. Words usually flow easily when I'm with my friends, but when I opened my mouth words refused to come out.

Clair sighed and pushed herself up from the floor. "I can explain." She took my arm and helped me up.

Mason stood on his hind legs to bat at the earring I held, but I lifted it out of his reach. "Cat, you have done enough. I think you should go home." I walked through the living room and opened the door. Mason obediently followed and marched out of Clair's house. "Go straight home." Mason is a good cat, but I knew he wouldn't really do as I said. I doubted he even understood me, but he left. I closed the door and returned to the sofa where Clair waited, her cell phone in hand.

She looked me in the eye. "I called Anita, and she's on her way over. I want to talk to both of you at the same time. You're my friends and deserve the truth."

We waited for Anita in silence. The only sound an occasional car passing on the street. It was the most awkward I'd ever felt in the company of my friend. Clair got up and put on a pot of coffee. While she was in the kitchen, I mentally ran through possible scenarios. Was Clair really the girl I went to high school with? Was she going to tell me, she killed Giles Gold? Had she always had homicidal tendencies? Was Clair Lane even her name?

I really needed some caffeine.

Anita and the coffee arrived at the same time. She didn't bother to knock, but walked straight in and sat in a side chair. "What's going on? Clair sounded upset. What's happened?"

While Clair handed us our mugs, I held up the earring for Anita to see.

She reached out and took it. "Where did you get this? Did you go back to the Java for it? I thought we agreed to leave it there."

I held my hot mug close. "As far as I know, the one I found at the motel is still on the counter at Ava's. The one you're holding seems to be its mate."

Anita's blue eyes flashed. "Now I'm confused. Where did you get it?"

I swiveled to gaze at Clair. It was time for her to explain to both Anita and me.

After a sip of coffee, she began. "I guess it's obvious this earring is mine, since Mason dragged it out of my jewelry box. And so is the one that Ava has next to her cash register." Clair paused to take a couple breaths. "I know this looks really bad."

Anita sat forward. "Yes, it does. It is bad. Are you the girlfriend?" She sucked in a breath. "You were in that hotel room with Giles Gold." Leave it to Anita to get to the point.

Clair put up a hand. "I let this go far too long. Should have confessed as soon as Lauren showed us the first earring. I promise you, I'm not a killer. And I wasn't having an affair with the man." Judging from the look of disgust, Clair was telling the truth.

I sat up straight and made my best attempt at being encouraging. "I'm sure Anita will agree we don't suspect you of murder. Or the affair either. Why don't you start at the beginning and tell us what happened?"

With another deep breath, Clair began. "This will sound crazy, but please believe me. It's the truth. I got a message from Giles through my website. He said he wanted to talk to me about the festival, but in person, not on the phone or by email. I did wonder why a blogger wouldn't be comfortable with email, but I said fine. After all, I wanted to meet him. Famous food blogger. I could post a selfie with him on my site. And I honestly thought he'd want to talk about the contest."

Clair took time to lift her mug and take a drink before she continued. "Giles, Mr. Gold, said he'd come to me. I thought it was a long trip and strange that he was arriving weeks before the Marshmallow Festival." She shrugged. "But he was the professional, and I figured he knew what he was doing."

It all sounded unbelievable to me, but I kept my thoughts to myself and drank my coffee.

As she spoke Clair's eyes seemed to look through us, not at the wall but into the past. "He phoned me as soon as he got into town. Such a charming man, and nice to talk to. I guess I was so flattered I wasn't thinking clearly when I went to his hotel room."

Anita gasped. "You what?"

"Don't look at me that way. I admit I was a little nervous, but remember it was me who contacted him in the first place. I'd asked him to judge the event."

Clair got up and walked around the room as she continued. "When I got to his room, there was a bouquet for me. You know how I love flowers. They were red roses." She stood and gazed out the window for a moment.

"It didn't take long for me to realize something was up. I asked him what he really wanted. And that's when things got weird. He said that after I'd contacted him, he checked out my social media pages, and couldn't help but fall in love."

Clair returned to the sofa and sat down. "You know the health and fitness photos I post. He had printed them all and created an album." She stared at me. "That wasn't normal, was it?"

I shook my head. "The man was unstable. Not that any man wouldn't fall in love with you, but Giles took it too far." I was floored. Gold must have been nuts.

She continued. "Well, when I finally realized he didn't want to talk about the festival, I tried to let him down nicely. You know, I still wanted him to judge the contest. Didn't want to make him mad. I told him I'd seen pictures of his wife on the blog and she seemed nice. I started talking about marriage being a sacred bond, and that he would be happiest if he went home and worked on his relationship with her."

Clair closed her eyes for a moment. "Guess that wasn't what he wanted to hear. His face turned red. Blood pressure must have skyrocketed. I sort of edged toward the door and was going to make a break for it, but he grabbed my hand to pull me back."

Anita bounded out of her chair to sit beside Clair. "Girl! He assaulted you?"

"Not at all. He wasn't rough or mean. But when I resisted, we fell onto the bed. I jumped up right away and he rolled off the bed onto the floor.

"He sat there begging my forgiveness. Poor man seemed stricken, and looked really pathetic, so I promised not to tell anyone."

Anita squinted at Clair. "You're sure he wasn't violent?"

With a small smile, Clair assured us. "It happened just as I told you. Now you know the truth. I was in his motel room, but he was alive and well when I left, except maybe being ready for a heart attack. He was so overweight. One of the pitfalls of being a food critique, I suppose."

Clair stood and smoothed her skirt. "I need more coffee." From the kitchen, she said. "I must have lost my earring in the tumble on the bed. Didn't know it was gone until I got home, and sure wasn't going back to look for it."

My cup was still almost full but cold, so I followed Clair for a warm-up.

She leaned against the counter. "Guess I should have shared the story with you right away. When I didn't hear from him again, not even to cancel his part in the contest, I figured he went back to New York. Let me tell you, I was as shocked as anyone when he turned up in the garbage."

We took our cups back to the sofa, and the three of us lounged in Clair's living room. We cradled our coffee mugs for a long time in silence. Anita spoke first. "We're right back where we started, aren't we?"

"Not quite." I glanced at my friends. "How many men do you know can keep a secret? Or better yet, what do you think a jealous wife would do if she knew?"

Chapter Fourteen

A t The Rare Curl, I was enjoying one of my few quiet moments. Rarity cleaned brushes and Stacey read a magazine when the front door swung open. The string of bells, attached to the handle, jangled me out of my private meditations. I struggled to get my feet off the desk while Rarity jumped out of her chair and marched to greet the unexpected guest.

"Gloria Belletrist, it's good to see you. How have you been?"

Anyone new to town would never guess the robust lady in our waiting room governed Evelynton's public library. When I think of a librarian, I tend to see a quiet, mild mannered woman. She would be wearing a conservative outfit. Maybe a twin sweater set. She would definitely wear sensible shoes, and her hair would be pulled into a bun. This was most likely from my childhood.

Today our librarian wore a striking teal shirt, jeans, and turquoise jewelry. Topping it off were cowboy boots and leather vest with fringe swinging almost to her knees.

"Life is fantastic. Worked all week to get the new spiritual wing open. I expect there will be lots of interest now that we have a murderer on the loose. People tend to get spiritual when they think about death."

"Oh dear, that incident has us all on edge, but I trust Evelynton's finest will get it cleared up before we know it." Rarity waved her hands. "Let's think about something more fun. What can I do for you today?"

Gloria put both hands in her hair. "This mop needs cutting and I haven't found the time to call for an appointment. So I thought I'd drop in while I was in the neighborhood."

Rarity retrieved a shampoo cape. "How about right now? I have just enough time, if you're free."

"Absolutely. Let's do it. And while I'm here, I'll kill two birds."

The comment startled me for a moment, until I reasoned she didn't really mean to use the gun she often carried.

"Needed to talk to you about the Marshmallow Festival." While Rarity commenced the shampoo, Gloria raised her voice to be heard above the running water. "Girls, I know we've all been distracted by the murder. And Clair, who was the driving force of our festival committee, has completely dropped the ball. Another week has gone by and the festivities are a week closer. Nothing has been settled about the promotions."

A better friend would have jumped to Clair's defense, but I had to admit she hadn't been herself lately. There had been no urgent meetings. No calls to action. Then I remembered that I had been given a project to work on, but couldn't recall what it was.

After wrapping Gloria's hair in a towel, Rarity planted her hands on her hips. "You're right, none of us have been thinking about the festival and it's such an important event. What can we do?"

"Fortunately for all of us, I've devised a plan."

Rarity grabbed a comb and tugged tangles from Gloria's hair. "Tell us what you're thinking."

Gloria swiveled her chair to face Rarity. "I've done more than think. I've taken action. Went to the print shop and ordered fliers offering a special gift to anyone who presents it at a business on Evelynton's Main Street. Every store on the street will come up with a little gift for each visitor on the day of the festival. I've phoned almost everyone." She pointed at Rarity. "You're one of the last on my list. Knew I'd be seeing you."

Rarity returned the styling chair to its original position and gazed at Gloria's reflection in the mirror. "That's a lot of gifts. I don't believe we have enough time to order anything in bulk."

Gloria pointed at her hair to encourage Rarity to continue combing. "That's the genius of my plan. Of course the restaurants will offer a sample of whatever they have entered in the marshmallow contest. So that's easy. And any business, who can't come up with an item, will hand out a card with an encouraging quotation, suitable for framing. The text will be spiritual, motivational, or an amusing line from a book. I can help with appropriate quotations. There are a ton of them in my arsenal."

I hadn't noticed Stacey listening, and was surprised she was interested in anything other than fashion magazines. But she shuffled closer to the librarian and raised her hand like a middle-schooler. "Oh, I know what I can do. I'll offer a free braid to everyone. I bet I can even wind the braid up to form the shape of a marshmallow. And I'll put a ribbon on it."

Rarity squinted at Stacey. "That's a nice idea. But would you have enough time? You'll have your regular customers, too. I wonder how many visitors we'll have."

My coworker's eyes grew wide. "Oh, gosh. I could be working all night. Let's cut the offer down to girls twelve and under. That'll be more fun anyway."

"Good idea. You'll have to make a poster explaining what they're getting."

Stacey gave a satisfied nod and glanced at Gloria. "And Rarity always has awesome quotations. There won't be any problem with that."

Gloria grinned. "That's the spirit!"

I glanced at the wall where Rarity's current mantra had been stenciled. 'Rejoice Always.'

Gloria pulled from Rarity's grasp once again, and turned to me. "Even Patricia thinks this is a great idea. Said she has a case of scarves that never sold. She's going to dust them off and give them to visitors."

With a hand on either side, Rarity gently directed Gloria's head so she faced the mirror. The librarian raised a finger. "By the way, the deadline for your commitment is tomorrow. I have to put in our order at the print shop. The cards will be done by next week. Fliers will be ready this afternoon."

She strained her eyes to glare at me while keeping her head still. "If you'd ever finished that book you were going to write, you could do readings at the library."

I pressed my lips together.

Gloria continued. "I'm getting a team assembled to distribute the fliers. I'll drive a stack of 'em to towns west of here. Stacey, do you mind driving north as far as the state line? There really isn't anything east. Patricia is taking the vicinity of Warrenton. She wants to go shopping anyway."

Gloria spent the rest of her time in the chair describing card stock and designs for the quotation cards. "So, we're in agreement?"

Three of us nodded. Stacey and Rarity looking forward to their contribution. Me, thankful I wasn't a business owner, and sort of thankful I didn't have to spend the festival days giving public readings.

~~

I stepped into the street to cross to Ava's Java, keeping an eye on traffic while I spoke to Anita on my cell. "Fine Women's Detective Agency we are. I've asked all over town and haven't discovered anything about Giles Gold's activities before his death. No one seems to have seen him. Except Clair. And we're keeping that quiet."

A rusted white pickup blasted their horn at me, and I hustled to the safety of the opposite curb. "You haven't come up with anything more. I say we put the investigation aside until after the festival."

I could hear Anita's sigh through the phone. "As much as I hate to say it, I agree. I've been helping prepare for the church bake sale that will run during the festival, but I thought you would be working on the case. You know, since you aren't involved in the festivities."

"I am involved. Rarity's kept me busy getting The

Rare Curl cleaned and organized. She wants to be ready for all the new visitors."

"What's she giving away? Maybe I'll stop over."

"She brought in a case of travel sized hair spray to pass out along with the quotation cards."

"Cool. I'll wait 'til the last day and see if she has any left."

I said goodbye and clicked off the phone, without telling my friend I was at the Java. The coffee shop wouldn't be crowded, and I wanted to be alone. Time to drink coffee and think about nothing.

My first thought of the morning had held the hope that all the stress of this case would magically melt away. I didn't care if we never found Giles Gold's killer. As long as Farlow didn't pin it on one of my friends, I'd be fine.

That didn't describe any mystery writer I knew. Guess I chose the right business, penning nice travel articles that would never scare the little old people who read them.

The lovely coffee aroma met me at the door. The earring was still beside the cash register. I should tell Clair to come in and say she lost it. She did, just not in the coffee shop.

I slid into my favorite table, content to bask in the atmosphere, and not worry about anything. Alone.

Ava cleared a table and ventured over to my haven.

"Do you mind if I sit a moment?"

"Of course not. Please do." I sorta did mind.

The barista let out a sigh and lowered herself into the chair across from me.

I guess, as Rarity would say, the Lord didn't have quiet time planned for me. "You seem troubled, Ava.

Anything wrong?"

She put her elbows on the table. "It's Konrad. He's after me to give up Ava's Java and retire. He's been harping on it since the murder. But now he's got it into his head that we should move out of town."

I stared at her. "Move? Away from Evelynton?"

"He said to another state. Maybe out west."

My heart started to race. "That's awful. What about your life here? Do you think the killing brought this on?"

Ava shrugged. "I suppose that's the main thing. I told him in a few months it would all be over and we could get back to normal. But he insisted we should have a new beginning." Ava put her hands palm down on the table and leaned toward me. "Imagine. A new start at our age! I don't know what's come over him."

My mind was whirling. "He can't mean for you to leave your home and friends. I bet he'll think about it and realize how painful that would be for you."

She shook her head. "I've given him plenty to think about, but the man is obsessed. Said that right after the festival, he wants me to talk to Clair about putting the shop on the market."

She glanced over her shoulder. "Gotta get back to work. Thanks for listening to me." Ava stood, slid her chair under the table, and scurried away to wait on customers. Poor Ava.

Poor me.

My favorite coffee spot would never be the same. No one could run it like Ava. Would she surrender her coffee recipes to the next owner? I gave myself a mental slap, and muttered. "Stop whining, Lauren. It's not about you."

Wait. What if new owners changed the Java? What if it wasn't even a coffee shop anymore? What if it became a hardware store or something? I ran my hands over the table top, cool, familiar. No more special seat by the window. What would Ava's loyal customers do? What would I do?

"Okay." I scolded myself. "You're being selfish. This is about Ava and Konrad, not you."

But why was Konrad acting that way? He'd always been strong, unflappable. He and Ava were innocent bystanders of this crime. Surely he knew it would be resolved soon. They would be fine.

Was he sure of it? I sympathized with Konrad's desire that his wife retire. She worked long hours. But why did he want to leave town? He had friends in Evelynton, too. What was he running from?

It seemed the Woman's Detective Agency was destined to meet again. Had anyone checked into Konrad's whereabouts on the night of the murder?

I cradled my precious mug of Ava's Killer Blend for a moment before I picked up my cell. Then, I sent texts to Anita and Clair calling a meeting. This time we would gather at one of our homes.

I hated my suspicion. If I was right, it would kill Ava.

Chapter Fifteen

Clair must have been watching for me. As soon as I pulled my 1975 Chrysler New Yorker station wagon into her driveway, she hustled out. While depositing her bag on the seat, she complained. "Don't know why you wanted to drive. I would have been happy to take the BMW." I waited while she leaned out again and put one foot on the concrete for leverage in wrestling the door shut.

When I thought she'd settled into the seat, I shifted into reverse and pulled into the street. "I like driving. There's no reason you and Anita always have to use your cars. Besides, the wagon has been a good ride, very reliable."

Clair still fidgeted in the seat. "There will be a day when it won't be reliable. You should be looking at used cars. Are these seat belts even safe? They have to be outdated."

"They're fine. I'm a careful driver and never drive fast enough to risk an accident."

Clair huffed. "That's not particularly reassuring. Anyway, what's the urgent meeting about? I thought we were taking a break from detective work."

I took a moment to maneuver the wagon onto a road that led out of town. "I think we need to rethink a suspect or two. And I'm afraid it isn't safe to wait. Let's talk when we get to Anita's so she won't feel left out."

Clair and I discussed plans for the Marshmallow Festival, but spent most of the three miles into the countryside in relative silence. My mind was occupied with thoughts of Konrad. Clair's must have been occupied with her mortality, since she kept rechecking the latch on her seat belt.

Anita's picture perfect farm house sat at the end of a long tree-lined drive. Neither she nor her husband farmed. Instead, they leased out the surrounding land to a soy bean grower.

I parked the car in front of a pristine white outbuilding I knew from experience was filled with snow mobiles and a barbecue grill. As we disembarked, two resident Labrador retrievers trotted over to welcome us. Clair made a fuss over them, with hugs and ear scratches. I gave each an awkward pat on the head and a "Good dog." After all, I'm a cat person.

At any rate, the dogs were kind enough to accompany us into the house. The younger of the two, a large chocolate brown beast, disappeared into the kitchen while his older brother sprawled out in the middle of the living room floor and began to snore.

We heard a welcome greeting from somewhere in the house, stepped over the dog, careful not to disturb him, and sank into Anita's comfy flowered sofa.

Our friend arrived from the kitchen with a tray of coffee. After serving, she backed up and plopped into an overstuffed arm chair. "What's up? Thought we were on hiatus? Don't get me wrong, I'm always up for an adventure. But why the change?"

I enjoyed a big slurp of my coffee, then took my time in relating the conversation with Ava. After I'd shared my suspicions, my friends stared at me with round eyes and open mouths.

Clair broke the silence first. "Konrad did it. Why would he want to leave town unless he had something to hide?"

Anita placed her untouched coffee on a side table. "Oh dear, who would ever suspect that nice man? Don't you think there's another explanation?"

Clair twisted toward Anita. "I suspect him. Obviously Lauren does too. What other answer is there?"

Blond curls bounced as Anita stood and paced around the room. "I don't know. But I'm sure there is one. Maybe family problems? Perhaps they have to leave to take care of a sick aunt."

Clair shot back an answer. "They don't have any family in the states. And if that were the reason, Ava would have told Lauren."

"Oh. Right."

Clair glanced at me. "We'll have to check on his alibi."

I nodded, drumming my fingers. "Did he have an alibi? I don't remember anyone saying."

Cell phone in hand, Clair began scrolling through her contacts. "Irma will know. She has access to the reports at the police department."

Anita had collected herself and returned to her seat. "Irma wouldn't technically be able to tell us about anyone's alibi, so we'll have to catch her in the right mood."

After a pensive sip of coffee, I offered the answer. "Let's ask her to lunch. She likes Burgers 'N Bean Sprouts. I bet she'll loosen up and talk then."

Anita, back in the game, offered, "While we're at it, we can ask if Farlow checked into the owner, Carl Rocco. I never discovered any real proof that he was working late the night of the murder." Cutting her eyes to Clair. "We got sidetracked by the earring."

~~

Standing at the door of Burgers 'N Bean Sprouts, I scanned the room. Clair and Anita had yet to arrive but I saw a menu seemingly standing on its own in a booth at the opposite wall. I suspected that would be Irma, the upper half of her body hidden by the board. Probably the tiniest adult in Evelynton, but what she lacked in size she made up in attitude.

"What looks good?" I slid across the red vinyl seat opposite Irma.

"Hey, Halloren. How's it goin'?" She dropped the menu on the table. "I decided I'll have sprouts on my burger today. I've always figured they were weird, but other people eat 'em. I'll give it a try. Where're the girls. My stomach's growling."

"Clair went to pick up Anita. They should be right behind me."

We heard Clair and Anita before we saw them. Their chatter grew louder as they walked through the restaurant. Irma and I scooted over, in our respective sides of the booth, to give them room.

Anita smiled at Irma. "So good to see you, Irma. How's Frank's indigestion?" I didn't remember that her husband was named Frank, and had no idea he'd had indigestion. Anita kept track of everyone.

"Frank's back to eating everything in sight." The diminutive woman handed both the newcomers a menu in a not-so-veiled attempt to hurry things along. "While we're on the subject."

Anita brightened. "I know what I'm having. A burger with everything, except no sprouts. And curly fries. I love them."

Clair put down the menu. "I want mine with sprouts. The Festival's coming, with all that rich food."

Small talk didn't last long. Irma was smart enough to know we were there to pick her brain about the investigation. She cut to the chase. "Farlow hasn't come up with anything. He doesn't have a clue as to who or why. All alibis have checked out. He can't discover a motive." She flapped a hand at us. "He's considering putting it down to a vagrant who must have wandered into town."

Clair shook her head. "Just wandered in, committed murder, and then what? Wandered out?"

Irma put up her hands. "Before you say anything, I know it's crazy. We haven't had a vagrant in town in— forever. Well we thought we did two years ago, but that one was explained after Halloren here solved the case."

I wanted to quash the myth that I'd solved any murder case, but the waitress arrived with our lunch, and proved how short my attention span is. "These are the best burgers in town. I wonder what makes them so good." I received only shrugs in reply. Everyone's mouth was full.

Anita waved a curly fry at Irma. "We've been thinking about alibis. Does everyone have one? Just take, for instance maybe, Konrad? Where was he?"

Irma sat back and squinted at Anita. "Just for instance? I'd have to check, but I think he said he was home with Ava all night."

Anita nodded. "Oh, I see. And did Ava corroborate that?"

"Who are you? Perry Mason? In answer to your question. Yes, as far as I know she agreed with him. Of course, being his wife, she would protect him. I mean if she thought he had anything to do with a murder."

I sat back in my seat. "So everyone has a husband or wife to confirm they were home on the night in question. Except Clair and me. I have Mason, but I doubt anyone would believe a cat. After all I feed him."

Clair shoved her plate away. "What about Melanie D'agastino?"

Anita jumped out of her seat, startling the waitress who had arrived to collect plates. "Oh, sorry Tina." She nailed Clair with intense blue eyes. "That little girl couldn't have done it. You know that."

Clair shrank back in her seat. "Sorry. She's not a little girl. She's a teenager, but I agree, she didn't do it. Just keeping the conversation going."

Irma shook her head. "Even Farlow says she's not the type. He's been studying criminal psychology."

This grabbed Clair's attention. "Is he taking classes at community college in Warrenton?"

Irma gave a loud guffaw and waved off the question. "Not hardly. His studies involve getting books from the library and watching cop shows."

I said, "That's nice. He's trying to better himself." I wasn't about to criticize him. His resources seemed to be the same as my resources in studies of the criminal mind.

Anita pulled her hand bag from the booth. "That's true. He could use some help in understanding people."

"Almost forgot." She leaned toward Irma and whispered. "I wonder. Did anyone check on Carl Rocco's alibi? We thought since he's in the contest..."

Another laugh spilled from Irma. "You girls are such fun. You're way outside of the suspect pool. Rocco wasn't anywhere near the place when the body was found. What reason would we have to ask him his whereabouts?"

Anita shrugged. "We thought maybe he wanted his friend, the mayor, to be judge instead of Gold."

This elicited a roar from Irma. "Like Farlow is going to pull in the mayor's friend for questioning, even if he was a suspect." She nudged Clair out of the way and scooted out of the booth. "Gotta get back to real police work. It's been fun. Let's do it again sometime." With that, Irma dropped her payment off at the cashier and left.

My friends and I, feeling thoroughly chastised, picked up our checks and filed to the cashier as well.

Carl Rocco happened to walk out of the kitchen in time to hold the door for us. "Good afternoon ladies. I trust you enjoyed your lunch."

Startled, we nodded like a trio of bobble head dolls. "Oh, yes. It was wonderful."

In the parking lot, Clair said, "We handled that like a bunch of clowns. Guilty clowns."

Anita stepped in close. "Did you see how he leered at us? Must have heard us asking about him."

Ever trying to bolster the troops, I said, "Did he? I wouldn't call it a leer. He was being nice. That's what owners do. You're feeling guilty since we talked about him."

Anita didn't seem convinced as she shuffled behind Clair to the BMW. I hurried to the wagon and glanced over my shoulder as I slid behind the wheel and turned on the engine. Movement caught my eye. Was that Carl Rocco peering from the restaurant window?

Chapter Sixteen

A quick jerk of the steering wheel saved me from landing in the ditch. Since leaving Burgers 'N Bean Sprouts, I'd almost lost control more than once, while swerving to avoid a mailbox. It isn't smart to drive with all one's attention centered on the rear-view mirror. I'd been convinced Carl Rocco was on my tail, so kept searching the road behind me. He wasn't. In reality there were no cars behind me at all. That revelation didn't give me peace, nor did it keep my attention on the road ahead.

Enough. I slammed on the brakes and pulled to the side of the road, needing a few minutes to calm down. And to convince myself I wasn't being followed by some murderous restaurant owner. I shifted into neutral, let the car idle, and practiced my deep breathing technique. Clair, the health fanatic, had shared the method with me. She seemed to think there were times I could use more self-control.

After a few minutes, my muddled brain began to clear. During that time no cars had passed me traveling in either direction. Unfounded paranoia confirmed.

While I enjoyed the moment of peace, I considered the case. What witnesses had I spoken to? What clues were uncovered that had been overshadowed by my obsession with Gold's supposed girlfriend, who happened to be Clair?

Shuffling through my memories of possible witnesses, Cheryl, the maid at E-Town Gardens, came to mind. She'd reported how surprised she was that her new friend Bob, i.e. Giles Gold, would steal from his room. Particularly an old, thread-bare blanket.

His online reputation didn't lead me to suspect him of petty theft. But what had happened to the blanket? Had they found one in the dumpster? In his rental car?

I glanced at the road ahead. A large dark sedan slowed as it drove toward me. Faces pressed to the window, ogling the stranded motorist as they passed. Crap. It was Clive and Murine Baron.

Before they could make a U-turn, I shifted into gear. The last thing I needed was my neighbor returning to ask if I'd had car trouble. Clive would have the Chrysler hood up before I had a chance to explain. With a quick check for traffic, I pulled the wagon onto the highway. Now to get home, sort my notes, and consider the implications.

Cruising through town, I saw Officer Farlow crossing the street, apparently on his way to the police station. I slowed. Should I stop? It seemed like fate. So easy to ask him about the blanket. Maybe not easy. A conversation with him was never a treat. But following the man into the station would be worse. He could show off for everyone by kicking me out.

I stopped in the middle of the street and lowered the window. "You-hoo, Officer Farlow."

He came to an abrupt stop and looked over his shoulder. Then, checking for oncoming traffic, he whirled and took a step toward me. Well, I suppose he recognized me, because he stopped.

With furrowed brow, he shouted. "What is it, Ms. Halloren?"

I put on what I considered an innocent smile. "Sorry to bother you. I see you're on your way to work, but if you could spare a minute." I was in luck. His rigid posture relaxed, so I charged ahead. "You know me. I can't help but think about the complexities of the murder. Not that I'm interfering or anything. I'm no investigator, but couldn't help but wonder. When Giles Gold's body was found in the dumpster, was there something out of the ordinary with it?"

Farlow looked at the sky for a moment, tilted his head down, and glared at me. "Woman, what are you talking about?"

Best not to take offense at his tone. "I know it's a silly question, but if you'll humor me. Was the body wrapped in anything, like a blanket?"

"As if it's any of your business, no." He leered at me. I sensed the rigidity returning. "There was no blanket keeping the poor corpse warm."

I took a breath and forced a chuckle. "I know he didn't need to be kept warm. He was dead. But I thought the killer might have wrapped the body in something before transporting it."

The mocking grin disappeared. Farlow's expression turned stern and threatening. "Listen. And listen carefully. I'm not discussing this case with you. Keep your nose out of police business, in this instance, and whatever murders you may stumble over in the future. I won't warn you again." Farlow pivoted and stalked to the curb.

I should have taken the cue. I should have stepped on the gas and sped away. But that hasn't been my nature in the past and apparently not the present either. My car still sat in the street when Farlow stopped and twisted toward me. I caught sight of his expression, and froze. After a moment, he walked back across the street and stood close to my window. He lowered his voice to a menacing rumble. "What makes you think the body had been moved? While you're here, Ms. Halloren, park your vehicle and come into the station. I want to talk to you."

Crap. "Why? I just thought it would have been difficult to kill the man inside the dumpster, so the killer had to have moved him." I squeaked.

"I'll see you in my office. Come in now, or I'll send a squad car for you." Farlow did an about-face and stalked up the stairs to the station.

A parking space opened just ahead, so I pulled the wagon into it. I sat for a moment, deep breathing again, until the trembling subsided. I coaxed the door open and followed the officer's instructions.

The door to Farlow's office stood open when I entered the station. He sat at his desk, staring at me. I walked in and sat in the chair across from him. I'd left the door open, on purpose. Farlow got up to shut it.

He still stood at the door when he said, "I remember you arrived late to the meeting at Ava's Java the day the body was discovered. Where were you the morning of the murder?"

I twisted to peer at him over my shoulder. "I was at home. All night. I was late to the meeting because my alarm didn't go off and I overslept. I told you all this before."

He'd reached his chair and pulled out a pad of paper. "Who can confirm your story?"

"Umm, no one. You know I live alone. Except for Mason, my cat."

"So, you have no alibi."

"Alibi? Why do I need an alibi? I didn't know the man and certainly had no reason to kill him."

Farlow leafed through his notebook. "It's come to my attention that you may have been acquainted with Mr. Gold. Contrary to what you may believe, we here at the department know how to investigate a crime. I talked to a workman at the hotel where Gold stayed. He described a woman who may have been in the area of Gold's room. That woman could have been you."

"No. You're wrong about that. Bud said the woman had short hair." Oops. I skidded to a stop, wishing I could swallow those words.

Farlow's beady eyes snapped at me. "So, you have spoken to the plumber. Maybe trying to sway his testimony? Possibly an attempt to keep him from reporting what he saw?"

"No! I was investigating. No, not investigating. I mean I happened to be at the motel and talked to him." I stopped. The room had begun to swirl around me. How did I get myself into this? I gripped the arms of the chair and breathed in to clear my head. "Anyway, if you interviewed him, you know he said the woman in question had short hair."

Farlow tipped back in his chair and wagged a finger at me. "Easy mistake. The way you wear your hair slicked back in that tail thing, looks like you have no hair at all."

I gasped and put a protective hand on my pony-tail. "Does not." I scooted out of my chair. "I'm not here to be insulted. Unless you're going to arrest me, I'm leaving. This is ridiculous and I have things to do at home." I slung my bag over my shoulder and wished I hadn't used the word arrest. Detain? No, that wouldn't have been a smart choice either.

"I'm not holding you now, but heed this warning." His eyebrows formed a straight black line. "Don't leave town."

"I have no reason to leave town." Flinging the door open, I scooted out.

As I made my escape to the outside world, I heard Farlow bellowing in the background. "Amos, that plumber at E-Town Gardens. Get him on the phone. Tell him to get in here. I want to talk to him again."

Chapter Seventeen

W hy did Jimmy Farlow always pick on me? After my meeting with him, I'd spent three days holed up in my house, avoiding everyone. Even called in sick one day. Introverts need quiet time, so for me this was a vacation.

In my sensible mind, I knew I was innocent and he would never find any proof I'd had anything to do with Gold's death. Farlow's interview with the plumber would prove I hadn't attempted to influence him. Why Farlow had me so spooked, I couldn't explain. Unless it was the badge, and the fact that what I'd done might be viewed as interference with police business. But no harm had been done.

Thank goodness, after this time of seclusion, I seemed to be outside the net Farlow was casting. Three glorious days and no further threats from him. No policeman had shown up at my door. No summons. No squad cars arriving to haul me away.

In these days of contemplation, I'd decided to forget all about Giles Gold, Konrad Kraus, and Carl Rocco. I'd called Clair and Anita to let them know I

117

was finished with the investigation. And had even tossed the newspaper in the trash without opening it, lest there be a story on the unsolved crime.

When I ventured back to the Java, I wouldn't even listen to gossip. Maybe I'd find the set of earbuds that fit my phone. With those in my ears, it would be easy to ignore everyone. I'd make it clear I didn't even want to know if the police accused one of my friends of homicide. As I thought about it, I figured there wouldn't be enough evidence to accuse anyone of anything. Farlow would be forced to give up. He would go back to chasing down parking violators and delinquent library fines.

I picked up my current novel and plopped on the sofa. I loved my house, doors closed and curtains drawn. Private. Quiet. Just me and my cat. Maybe I'd stay home a few more days.

Unfortunately, and realistically, I would be forced to leave my sanctuary. Today I would go to work at The Rare Curl, but planned to stay firm in my resolve and remain ignorant of police activities.

~~

I swung the salon door open, listening to the sweet jingle of the bells. Stacey glanced up from her styling chair, where she chatted with a customer. Rarity emerged from the back room, hauling a ladder. Gladys, the cleaning woman, followed her, carrying a bucket and mop.

Rarity sang a hearty hello. "Tomorrow is the big day, so we're doing a final cleansing and polishing of the shop. Gladys was good enough to take time from her busy schedule to give us a hand." I tucked my handbag away and took my place at the reception desk.

While Rarity positioned the ladder and climbed it to fiddle with the track lighting, Gladys swiped the mop around the shampoo bowls. As was her habit, the charwoman maintained a constant narrative. "I bet you'll get a lot of visitors, just wanting to see your shop. People recognize an honest business when they see it. Nobody has ever said a bad word about you, Rarity. Everyone knows you're a good woman."

Rarity, at the top of the ladder, called, "That's kind of you, Gladys." She pointed to the floor. "I dropped my rag. Would you toss it to me?"

The cleaning woman propped the mop against a shampoo chair, grabbed the rag and gave it a toss to Rarity. "I'm not sure the festival is a good thing. Just hope it doesn't bring in the wrong sort. There's bound to be a bad element. Thieves and so on. We've got our own trouble makers. Sure don't need to invite outsiders in."

She took a minute to rinse the mop. "It gets to me when I see even our own people taking advantage of what isn't theirs. Did I tell you what I witnessed a couple weeks ago? Right over there, beside Ava's. I was on my way to work. It was still dark, cause I had to get my cleaning done before the insurance office opened for business."

Gladys propped the mop again and planted her fists on her hips. "I was driving down Main Street when I saw it. There was somebody sneaking around, so I watched them. Turns out they were out to get free dumpster service. There were two of them and they carried a load of garbage into that alley over there. Stuffed a big bag into the can, as if they owned it. Ava has to pay for that service. It was obvious they knew they weren't supposed to, else why would they have been sneaking around in the dark?"

Rarity unscrewed a light bulb. "Now Gladys, maybe it was Ava getting ready for the day."

"Nope. It sure wasn't Ava or Konrad. I know them. These two…"

Rarity held out the bulb. "Gladys, can you help me with this light fixture. Let's put all the bulbs in the sink and wash them. They'll shine brighter, and everything in the salon will look cleaner."

I tried to be like Rarity and think about only good things. Gladys's words rang in my brain. I covered my ears and reminded myself I wanted nothing to do with crime. But my thoughts made a beeline to murder.

I spun my chair away from the desk. "Gladys, when was it that you witnessed somebody using the dumpster?"

The cleaning lady stood with her finger to her chin. "Let me think."

Rarity's ladder shuddered. She clung to it and raised her voice. "Grab this before I take a tumble."

Gladys ambled over to help Rarity, saying as she went, "I don't really recall, been working a lot of hours. A week or two. Maybe three." She flapped a hand at me. "I don't remember. All I know is there's dishonest people in this world. Things like that happen often enough in Evelynton on ordinary days. We don't need to be inviting outsiders in."

Gladys reached out and steadied Rarity's ladder.

I heard my boss quietly reciting, "Whatever is true, whatever is noble, whatever is…"

Rarity was right. If I pursued this, I'd likely get myself into trouble. The phone rang and I spun my chair back to the desk to answer it.

By the time my shift had ended, I'd all but forgotten Gladys's revelation.

Chapter Eighteen

The Rare Curl shone. Retail shelves dusted, floors cleaned, fresh flowers on the reception desk and next to them a stack of quotation cards-suitable for framing, completed the spiffy presentation. Stacey, with a handful of ribbons, could barely contain her excitement at the thought of greeting little girls who wanted a special braid. I stood at the door, handbag slung over my shoulder, admiring the salon. "Everything sparkles. The Rare Curl is ready for visitors."

"Thanks for helping us get set up. Now go and have a good time at the Marshmallow Festival. I'm sure we can handle everything, but I'll give you a call in the unlikely event we get swamped." Rarity pointed to the crowd passing on the sidewalk outside. "Just look at all the people on the street already this morning."

I had to admit being impressed by the interest. "The town council owes Gloria Belletrist a big thank you. She's a marketing genius. I never thought anyone other than local residents would be interested in a festival for marshmallows."

Rarity waved a comb at me from her styling chair where her first client of the day sipped her coffee. I gave a quick flap of my hand and a "Have a good day" as I slipped out to the sidewalk.

I felt as free as if I'd skipped school. Tampa had never had a festival in the twenty years I lived there. Or maybe they did and I'd never been interested. As this was the first Marshmallow Festival in Evelynton for several years, the whole town throbbed with excitement.

I slid in among the horde of early arrivals. Vendors lined Main Street. Peddlers set up tables with every kind of jewelry, pottery, painting, and craft item. There were necklace and earring sets with marshmallow dangles, pottery with marshmallow etchings, and paintings of roasted marshmallows over campfires.

On the far side of the barricades, a continuous stream of humanity filed in from streets lined with parked cars. As a people watcher, the men, women, and children, proved equally as fascinating as the arts, crafts, and sugary treats.

I scanned the arrivals, searching for familiar faces. Clair would be among the festival goers distributing her business cards along with the quotation gift card.

I remembered Anita had volunteered to assist Ava in serving samples of her brownie treats. Konrad would certainly have been put in charge of crowd control due to the recent notoriety of the Java.

A block past The Rare Curl, a side street was reserved for edible concessions. Every food tent and truck was required to contain real marshmallows in some way. I'm sure they all complied, even if the corn-dog was served with a marshmallow on the side. I predicted a cloud of sugar buzz would soon settle over Evelynton.

I found Anita leaving a truck advertising five kinds of smores. Who knew there were different kinds? "Smores already?"

Anita licked each finger before answering. "I'm calling it breakfast. The festival doesn't come around often, so I intend to experience as much as possible. I'm due at the Java in a bit, but I have time for coffee before checking in. Join me?"

I watched melting chocolate seep over the graham cracker and onto her hand, thinking that was too much sugar for me to think about before lunch. "Absolutely."

At the counter, I ordered black coffee. Anita asked for the same. I scanned the room, looking for a seat while Anita added three sweeteners and cream to her cup.

I tipped my head toward the counter. "I see Melanie is back to work."

"She is such a nice girl, and brave to come back here. She didn't want to leave Ava in the lurch during the festival."

We nabbed a table only one row away from our favorite window seat. Anita pointed to the mass of festival goers on the sidewalk. "There's Clair." She leaned across the unfortunate couple seated next to the window, and pounded on the pane until Clair caught sight of her. Our friend reversed direction, fighting the traffic flow back to the Ava's Java entrance. After a stop at the coffee counter, Clair joined us.

"Only have time for a quick cup. Along with passing out business cards, I'm on vendor patrol to confirm everything is marshmallow related." She opened her cross-body purse. "Did you see my quotation card? Of course Rarity came up with the perfect text. '**A house is made with walls and beams. A home is made with love and dreams.**' Isn't it perfect? Makes me want to cry." She wrapped her hands around the mug and sipped. "I think I'll call Michael and ask him to come over for dinner tonight."

Michael Barry, the local veterinarian, had been seen escorting Clair to dinner, during the past year. Most of us agreed he seemed to be smitten with her. But our professional friend, tended to avoid commitment.

Anita smiled. "When will you put the man out of his misery? I bet he would like to make your relationship official."

Clair avoided eye contact. "Yes, I think he would."

She chugged her coffee. "Gotta go." With a wave, she strutted out to the street as fast as her four inch heels would carry her.

Anita watched Clair merge with the festival goers on the street. "That was fast. I guess I shouldn't have brought it up. You both think I'm always trying to get you to settle down."

"We know you want us to be happily married like you are. Clair seems to be moving closer to that blissful state, but don't expect it of me."

"What's going on with your handsome ex-FBI agent? I haven't heard you talk about him for a while.

"I won't be talking about him, at least not to say anything nice. He's much too busy with his consulting firm to think about me. I haven't heard from him in weeks."

Anita shrugged. "I guess it wasn't meant to be.

Someday someone better will show up and we'll understand why it didn't work out with Jack."

I fought the urge to roll my eyes. "Uh, huh." I pointed at the coffee counter. "I think it's time for you to go to work."

"Yikes." She downed the last dregs in the cup. "You're right. Look at the line. I'm supposed to be handing out samples of Ava's Killer Fudge Marshmallow Brownies."

Killer Fudge? Was that a clever advertising ploy? Or an unfortunate choice of names?

~

My next stop was Patricia's dress shop. I was interested in how the left-over scarf gifts would be received. A glance through the front window made it clear her business would benefit from the festival. The racks were crowded with browsing women. I mingled with the shoppers and inched close to the counter. Moving forward, prodded and jostled, I finally found a spot within a few feet of the proprietress.

Patricia stood behind a box piled high with multi-colored bandanas. Her voice carried above the din. "These are the latest fashion accessory, ladies. You'll see them in all the magazines." She held one up to the closest customer. This one's perfect for you, dear. The shade makes your eyes sparkle."

Were they the latest thing? It couldn't be proved by me. I hadn't picked up a fashion magazine in years, or ever.

The dress store proprietor caught sight of me, so I flashed a smile and a wave, hoping to signal that I understood she was too busy to chat. I reversed direction and fought my way out of the congested store.

If it were possible, the street outside was more claustrophobic than the dress shop. The population of Evelynton must have tripled for the day. I wouldn't have guessed so many people would be interested in our little burg, with or without marshmallows.

Moving along with the throng, taking short steps to avoid treading on heels, I looked for an escape route. My hope was that the mass would thin out by the time we reached the food alley. The spirit of the festival must have been seeping into me, because I found I was ready for breakfast. The sugary kind. Maybe I'd begin with Marshmallow Waffles. After that, possibly a sample of each variety of smores.

My mouth, watering and hungering, pushed me forward, when my attention was diverted by blond hair, severely fastened in a chignon, above a pudgy woman's body. Cravings pulled me back to the waffles until I noticed the woman's companion. Portly man with a donut hair style. I pushed forward until I confirmed the identity of Rosemary and Sage Gold.

Why had they returned to Evelynton? They certainly hadn't been complimentary to our town. Were they festival fanatics, or just plain fanatics, that they would visit the place their father was killed? I followed as they fought their way to the head of every line, moving from food truck to food truck. Watching them eat became tedious, and I was about to return to my own breakfast search when things got interesting. Rosemary grabbed Sage's ear and motioned into the crowd. I gazed in the direction of her pointing finger, but saw only strangers and the hot chocolate wagon. The two Golds walked determinedly in that direction. Maybe they were only thirsty, but I followed.

Keeping them in my radar wasn't easy while dodging ice cream cones, smores, and hot drinks. As I attempted to circumvent a little white-haired woman and a cluster of children, the Golds took a hard left. I'd missed the turn before I applied the brakes, but fought my way back. Where were they heading? I'd have been extremely disappointed if their destination was another food truck.

Searching the crowd, trying to anticipate the route to their destination, I discovered the target. Clair Lane stood in their direct line of fire. Blissfully distributing business cards, and unaware of danger closing in.

Like a small pack of wolves on the hunt, the two Golds stalked progressively closer. I yelled, but my warning faded into the hubbub of the crowd. I tried to send psychic messages of approaching peril, to no avail.

At last, Clair glanced up and caught sight of Rosemary and Sage, and raised her eyebrows. Then she froze, undoubtedly staring into the demon eyes of her pursuers.

Clair suddenly pivoted and dashed into the crush of bodies. The Gold kids plowed forward like a pair of land movers. My athletic friend should have easily outrun the two, but for her high heels and the clutch of festival fans.

Clair made an error in judgment in her escape route and ran up against a brick wall. She cut to the left but was trapped by the Corn-Dog food truck.

I stumbled my way through the crowd and got close enough to hear Rosemary screech. "Get her! She's the one! She seduced my daddy."

Clair shook her head and shouted. "Noooo. I didn't!"

Rosemary shrieked. "You did! I found your pictures on Daddy's computer. It's your fault he died. If it wasn't for you, my daddy would never have been in this horrible, forsaken place."

Peering through the throng, I concluded Clair had been overcome by a convulsion. Her head vibrated back and forth. Her face was a blur. Business cards flew in all directions, and her purse fell to the ground. I thought epileptic seizure, but with further scrutiny, decided that wasn't it at all. Rosemary had latched on to Clair's arm and was shaking her violently. "You will pay for what you did to our family."

As Clair's head was being flung side to side, she let out a scream that rivaled the town fire alarm. Driven by the piercing cry for help, I pushed through the final few people obstructing my approach, and reached for my friend. After a failed attempt to obtain Clair's release, I debated whether to jump on Rosemary's back or continue the attempt to pry open the vise-like grip.

Before I'd reached a decision, Officer Farlow lunged into the fight. He grabbed Rosemary in a valiant effort to unlatch her from Clair. The woman was a whirlwind and proved too much for Farlow. A swift backhand caught him off guard and sent him sprawling on the ground. This convinced her to let go of Clair, and with a guttural cry, she leapt on top of Farlow. "You're supposed to be the law, and you should have helped us. When all the time you were protecting this woman."

The few bystanders who had noticed the scuffle, backed away, still eating their sweets.

I waited for someone to come to Farlow's aid, but decided I was the only one thinking along those lines, so I leapt into the fray, grabbing Rosemary's arm and pulling as hard as I could. Farlow was no match for her, so obviously I was out-gunned as well. She tossed me aside like a used candy bar wrapper. Then Clair appeared beside me, and between the two of us, we hefted Rosemary from the flailing lawman. The woman had yet to run out of steam. Clair and I, still clutching her arms, were being thrown around like rag dolls.

On one fling to the side, I thought to look for Sage. He stood on the sidelines munching on marshmallow nut bread. It seemed he wanted no part of the scuffle.

At long last, the posse arrived. Officer Smith moved in with his handcuffs. Gloria, our librarian, stood behind him, wide eyed and gun drawn.

Smith glanced at her. "Thanks Mrs. Belletrist. I've got it. Put away the weapon." Grabbing one chubby arm at a time, he managed to restrain Rosemary. He lifted her, yellow blond hair askew, to her feet.

I lay on the asphalt for a moment to catch my breath. Then I pushed my hair from my eyes and righted myself. Taking Clair's elbow, I helped her up, impressed that her suit was only slightly dusty and her shoes were still on her feet, though scuffed.

Gloria stood frozen in place still pointing her gun, so I whispered. "It's okay Gloria. You can put that away." She blinked at me. I thought she might be stunned from the excitement. But after a moment, she stowed her gun, backed up, and faded into a group of bystanders.

Farlow had yet to move from where he lay, sprawled on the street. I attracted Clair's attention, and together we helped him to his feet.

Having finished his nut bread, Sage stepped in.

"Don't hurt her officer. She's had way too much caffeine today. Happens every time. It makes her go berserk."

The Gold kids' mother, Ophelia, had wandered up to find her children in the middle of the commotion. She seemed calm for someone whose daughter was in handcuffs. "Rosemary, dear, how many espressos did you drink today?"

Rosemary shrugged. "Only four."

"I thought we agreed we wouldn't set foot in that coffee shop."

Sage glanced at his mother. "She had them at the bed and breakfast before we left. And I counted six."

Rosemary shot him a look. "Tattle tale."

Meanwhile, Farlow had brushed himself off, straightened his shirt, and pulled a notebook from his pocket. "Name?"

I couldn't help myself. Still hadn't caught on to keeping my thoughts to myself. "Really, Officer Farlow? You know her name. It's Rosemary Gold. You talked to her when her father was found murdered in the alley beside Ava's Java."

Farlow let out a loud, dramatic sigh. "Let her answer for herself. And keep out of this. You have nothing to do with it."

"Really? You call keeping you from being beat to a pulp nothing? You didn't have a chance against...."

Farlow shot a glare in my direction that did the trick to shut me up. Then he turned his attention to Sage Gold. "As I recall, you are this lady's brother."

"Yes sir. I am. And this is our mother, Mrs. Ophelia Gold."

"What instigated the attack on Miss Lane?"

"Caffeine, Officer."

Farlow's notetaking paused. "What?"

Ophelia stepped in, fluttering unnaturally long lashes. "It's the espressos, Officer. The devil's brew. I'm afraid it happens every time. My baby has some kind of allergic reaction, after four or five. You can see that it's a medical condition. And now that she's worked out the aggression, there's no reason to arrest her."

"Of course there's a reason. She assaulted this woman, and resisted an officer of the law. That's a serious matter." I was feeling sort of proud of Jimmy Farlow for standing up to the haughty woman.

Sage took up the pleading. "What if we promise to limit her intake? I'm so sorry we let her get this far. Should have known. The same thing happened when we came to visit...."

He pressed his lips together and stared at his sister before continuing. "The thing is we know it's a problem, and I promise to personally keep an eye on her, going forward."

Farlow slapped his notebook shut. "Tell it to the judge. I'm booking her. Take her in, Amos."

He turned to Clair. "I witnessed the assault. Come down to the station to fill out a complaint. We'll get this tied up in no time."

Although firmly held in Amos's grip, Rosemary gave a threatening lurch at Clair. My friend stumbled backwards. "Officer Farlow, I'd rather wait until she's locked up. Can't I go home now, and file the complaint tomorrow?"

"I said today!" Without waiting for a reply, and without thanking us for our heroic assistance, he followed Officer Smith and Rosemary from the food alley. Sage put an arm around his mother's shoulders, and the two trailed after Farlow.

Chapter Nineteen

Clair slumped against the corn-dog truck, her red tipped fingers tracing slow circles at her temples. "That woman rattled my brains and gave me a headache. I know Farlow insisted I get down to the station to file a complaint, but I just want to go home and take a few aspirin. Then maybe I'll spend the rest of the day on the sofa. I'd rather forget this whole ordeal."

I sure couldn't blame Clair for wanting to put it behind her. But what benefit is a past like mine, if not to offer advice to a friend? "I understand your reluctance, but take it from me you don't want Officer Farlow mad at you. Go in and get it over as soon as possible so it won't be hanging over your head."

Clair raised puffy eyes to me and let out a low groan.

I took a breath. I could make the trip more palatable, if I was a good friend. I spit out the offer before I changed my mind. "I'll go with you for moral support."

Clair's hands slapped her thighs as they fell to her sides, and gratitude splashed across her face. "I would love that. Thank you. You've been there and know what to expect."

Clair was aware of my police station phobia, so I'd hoped she would be grateful but assure me she was fine to go alone. Judging from the grin on her face, that wasn't going to happen.

"It's no problem at all," I said as cheerfully as I could.

Actually it might be a treat to be at the police station without occupying center stage. As a simple bystander, Farlow had no reason to suspect me of criminal activity.

Clair pushed herself away from the food truck and brushed some debris from her shirt. While she primped, my pocket vibrated. I pulled out my phone to find Anita's picture on the front. As soon as I answered, she said, "Get over to the Java right away. Something's going on."

I said, "Sure." and hung up.

"That was Anita. She wants to see us at Ava's Java." I flashed a smile at Clair. "We can get a coffee while we're there."

"Great. I'm feeling better already." She grabbed my arm, and together we wove our way through the crowd until we arrived at the Java.

Anita waved and motioned us over to where she stood beside the counter. "You've arrived at the perfect time. We've been rushed for the last fifteen minutes, but things have slowed down a little."

"What's up?"

She pointed at an empty table. "Take that table. I'll bring you some coffee and tell you about it."

Clair moaned. "I wish we could, but we can't stay."

"Just two cups of Ava's Killer Blend, to go." I described the turmoil in the food alley, adding Clair's summons to the station.

"Oh, poor thing." Anita put an arm around Clair in a hug, and then slid behind the counter. She handed us each a cardboard cup of java.

Clair wrapped her hands around her to-go cup and sucked in a big drink of the steaming liquid. "So, what's going on here?"

"It's Konrad. I've been keeping an eye on him all morning, since he's our prime suspect in the murder. All seemed to be going well, until a little while ago. He snapped at Ava and stormed out the front door. Ava seemed really flustered. She put Melanie in charge of the cash register, and she left. Without another word." Anita glanced at the counter. "I couldn't believe they both took off, since we've been so busy with the festival crowd."

Our friend kept an eye on the door and wrung her hands as she spoke. "Oh shoot. It's picking up again."

A creak of a door drew our attention to the kitchen entrance. Ava entered and hustled to the coffee counter. Anita sighed. "Praise the Lord, she's back. I didn't know what we were going to do for the rest of the day."

Ava took her place at the cash register and shouted to the customers in line. "Sorry, everybody. Had some pressing business to attend to. All fixed now."

Anita scooted into her place beside Ava, where she took charge of the Killer Marshmallow Brownie samples. Clair and I followed and hovered nearby.

As Ava mixed a specialty coffee drink, Anita leaned toward her, "Are you alright? Konrad ran out sort of suddenly. And when you left too, I was worried."

Ava handed the coffee to a customer. "Everything's fine. It's even better than fine. I wish he'd picked a better time, but Konrad finally blurted out what has been on his mind. You know we haven't talked much since he told me he wanted to sell the Java."

Anita, Clair, and I nodded and leaned in.

"It seems he was having a little mid-life crisis. You know men. He was afraid I was working too hard and, being the man of the family, thought it was his duty to help me. So he worked his own job, and whenever he had free time he thought he had to take over the management of the Java. The problem is, he never consulted me."

Clair raised her eyebrows. "Oh. Oh. I bet that didn't go over well."

Ava chuckled. "No it didn't. I've been running this place just fine for a long time. When I understood why he was acting so strangely, I told him that I respect him for wanting to help. But I didn't need it. I love my work. In fact, I thrive on it."

I agreed with Ava, since she continued to wait on customers as she talked to us. "All the extra customers today sent him over the edge. But I convinced him I can handle it. Sent him home. I need his support and encouragement but not his presence in my shop."

Anita said, "Was that why he was so insistent that you sell Ava's Java? We thought...."

Clair and I cut our eyes to Anita, successfully silencing her.

Ava chuckled. "For some reason he thought I'd be happier retired. Silly man. It took me a while, out there in the alley, but I convinced him to recognize this is my life, and I wouldn't have it any other way. So, he's decided to stop trying to be in control. In our marriage we are a team with individual roles to play."

I snatched a Killer Marshmallow Brownie sample from the tray. "I'm glad Konrad understands." Popping it into my mouth, I mumbled. "Hmmm. This town wouldn't be the same without you and the Java."

Anita walked with us to the door. "Guess I'll scratch Konrad off my suspect list. Darn. Not that I wanted him to be the killer, but I thought we had it solved."

Clair and I waved good-bye and carried our to-go cups of Killer Blend out into the crowd.

We took our time covering the three block trek to the police station sipping coffee and dodging countless people browsing the vendors instead of watching where they were going. I'd lost interest in the festivities, contemplating, instead, the seriously disturbed woman who had assaulted my friend. Clair remained quiet and didn't pass out a single business card.

When we arrived at our destination, I let Clair take the lead into the building. I followed close behind, so when she put on the brakes. I slammed into her. "Sorry."

She whispered to me. "Who are all those people?"

I peeked over her shoulder. "I have no idea."

The room seemed unusually congested, with men and women milling about in the waiting area and peeking into other rooms. At the center, Officer Amos Smith stood with Rosemary Gold, still wearing handcuffs. Sage and Ophelia Gold were at the side, squaring off with Officer Farlow. Everyone in the room witnessed the tirade as they repeated the defense Sage had used in the food alley. "It was a momentary lack of judgment, brought on by a slight medical condition. The whole silly thing was caused by the caffeine. Nothing to worry about now."

A group of strangers had congregated on the far side of the room. None of them were familiar to me. I concluded they were visitors in town for the festival. They must have witnessed the arrest and followed the action to the police station. In their eyes, this was probably an exciting mystery event, put on for the festival. A couple of them snapped pictures.

Irma stepped out of an adjoining office toting a stack of files. She spied Clair and me. "Hey, girls. How's the festival?"

We didn't answer, but Clair's pitiful expression seemed to convey our thoughts. The clerk scoped out the surrounding activity and carried the files into another office without further comment.

While Clair and I stood back waiting for Amos to lead Rosemary away, hopefully to a cell, a door opened behind us. I looked over my shoulder to see Evelynton's librarian, Gloria Belletrist enter the room. Judging from her glassy-eyed stare, I feared she was in distress. I whispered, "Are you okay? What are you doing here?"

Gloria lifted her shoulders and whimpered something indecipherable.

I concluded the woman was experiencing some kind of emotional episode. "Maybe you should go back to the library and rest."

She gave a vigorous shake of her head. "No, I have to confess."

Was it a mental break? "What would you confess? You must be disoriented. I can understand, with all the excitement down at the food alley. Would you like me to call someone to pick you up?"

This time her voice was strong enough for the entire room to hear. "I'm here to confess to the murder. I killed Giles Gold."

I slid back a couple steps. All conversations halted. The Gold clan snapped to attention. A few of the strangers procured more pictures.

Gloria squared her shoulders. "Officer Smith told me the death was thought to be by blunt force trauma, with cookie dough. I'm here to say I supplied the murder weapon. It was my dough."

The only sound in the room was the shuffling of Officer Farlow's shoes as he pivoted toward her, notebook and pen in hand. He opened his mouth, seemed to reconsider, and closed it.

Several scenarios played out in my mind featuring Gloria pelting Giles Gold with raw cookies. None of them believable. Someone had to save the woman. I returned to her side. "You're over-excited. Maybe we should get a cool cloth for your forehead."

But Gloria seemed to be gaining control of her emotions. She glanced at me and huffed, "Move aside and let me explain."

"Giles Gold came into the library looking for a street map. I love his blog and recognized him right away. Him, standing in my library was such an honor, I could hardly contain myself. I probably talked his ear off." Gloria grinned at all of us as she shared her good fortune. "Well I just had to tell him about the cookies my grandmother used to bake, and how I'd been tweaking the ingredients for years. I'd perfected the flavor, but never shared them with anyone. The right time had finally presented itself." Gloria paused and scanned our faces.

I'd pulled out my phone, considering a call to Emergency Services, when she continued her story. "As luck would have it, I had a roll of the dough in my freezer, so I ran right home and got it."

The librarian took a breath and beamed as she continued. "I presented it to Mr. Gold as a gift. He was very grateful, and promised to bake it and to write a review of my cookies on his blog, as soon as he returned to New York. He took it with him when he left the library."

Farlow blinked. "Mrs. Belletrist, thank you for that interesting story, but I'm not sure it implicates you in the death of Giles Gold." He shifted his gaze to me, standing in the unfortunate position beside Gloria. "I should have known. Halloren, what nonsense have you put into her mind?"

I raised my hands as a shield and shook my head. "This is all new to me. I'm just as surprised as you are."

The officer raised his arm, index finger pointing to the door. "Take the poor woman home."

I wasn't about to argue with him, and prepared to escort Gloria out, when a breeze blew into the room.

We all turned to see Gladys propping the door open with her hip and dragging in a bucket of cleaning supplies. The cleaning woman straightened and gazed at us. "What's going on in here? I thought the place would be empty with most of the police force out patrolling the streets. Is this a good time to clean?"

About this time I'd concluded I was still at home in my bed, and the whole day was a strange twisted nightmare.

Gladys scanned the room, taking in each person until her eyes landed on Rosemary and Sage Gold at the side of the room conferring with their mother.

The charwoman's mouth dropped open. "That's them. The crooks." Gladys advanced on Farlow. "Arrest those two. They're dumpster thieves. I know, because I witnessed the crime. They dumped garbage into a dumpster without authority. It wasn't theirs to use. The can belonged to Ava's Java."

Officer Farlow closed his eyes for a moment and shook his head. "We have more pressing matters here than unlawful garbage can use."

Gladys waved an index finger in Farlow's face. "That's the problem with the world today. You think some crimes are less important, and won't take the trouble to investigate. That's how it happens. Today the dumpster, tomorrow a terrorist attack."

Farlow rolled his eyes. "Gladys, we don't need your hysterics. Go home. You'll have to clean the station at another time." Having dismissed Gladys and Gloria, he returned his attention to Ophelia Gold.

If this wasn't a dream, there were two women in the room who might be having mental breakdowns. I put an arm around Gladys and guided her toward the door. I attempted to coax Gloria to accompany us, but she wasn't as cooperative. I needed to reconsider my approach with her.

As I neared the door, Officer Farlow twisted toward us. "Thank you for helping with them, Lauren."

I froze and stared at the lawman. Farlow had never thanked me for anything, and he'd never used my first name. Didn't know he was aware I had one.

At this point I had no doubt that the entire day had been a dream. What do you do when in the middle of a dream? Play along.

Chapter Twenty

Gladys followed me willingly. Gloria was made of sterner stuff. Even after my best persuasion, she planted her feet and refused to budge. I remembered she still had a gun on her, so thought it best to leave her where she was comfortable.

Outside, the washer woman made it halfway down the steps before she refused to go farther. Using my sweetest voice, I tried to convince her to leave the area. The only response I got was a tirade of police incompetence.

Finally, she spat out, "I won't be silenced!" and escaped my grasp to trudge back into the police station.

I briefly considered going home, but Clair was still inside and I'd promised to stay with her. Truthfully, the action inside was a lot more inviting than the safety of my house, so I couldn't resist following Gladys.

Inside, the Golds argued with Officer Smith. Gladys charged at Farlow with her arm raised, pointing at Sage and Rosemary. I searched the room for Clair, and found her hiding behind Gloria. The strangers at the far wall still snapped pictures. I watched the crazy episode play out and tried to stay out of the way.

Sometimes I'm a little slow, but while I studied the players—still thinking it might be a dream—pieces of the puzzle began to fit together. I left my safe space and stepped over to Sage and Rosemary. "Sorry to interrupt, but it was you at the dumpster, wasn't it? What were you doing?"

They turned to me with open mouths and stuttered simultaneously. "We weren't there."

I said, "Gladys is pretty certain it was you. Are you sure you didn't decide to use the dumpster to clean out your car, maybe throw away some fast-food bags?"

Sage raised his fist and blurted, "I said we weren't there. Why are you listening to that old woman? She's probably blind."

Gladys had followed me and hung over my shoulder. "Don't call me an old woman, I know what I saw. My eyesight is 20/20."

"But…." Sage caught his breath and hung his head. After blowing out enough air to deflate a large balloon, he glanced at his sister. "I'm sorry, Rosemary. I can't deny it any more. I tried, but keeping our secret is too heavy a burden."

Rosemary shook her head. "What secret? There's no secret. I don't know what you're talking about."

Perspiration had formed on Sage's forehead. "The woman saw us. The truth was bound to come out sooner or later. It's best we tell the truth now."

He locked eyes with Officer Farlow, and put his hands up in surrender. "Officer, it was my sister and me at the garbage can, but we weren't dumping garbage."

He pulled in a deep breath. "It was our father's body. Rosemary killed him. I'm telling you because I know it wasn't her fault. She had one of her medical episodes that caused her to fly off the handle. You saw one of them, so you understand."

Rosemary shot a glance at Farlow. "Don't listen to him. He's delirious."

Ophelia Gold gasped. "Sage Gold, why would you accuse your sister? I don't understand." She pulled a wad of tissues from her handbag and staggered to a chair at the side of the room.

Sage followed his mother and hovered, fanning her with his hand. "Mother, think about it. You know I'm telling the truth."

Ophelia turned red-ringed eyes to her daughter. "Is it true? Is that what happened?"

Rosemary gazed at the floor and huffed. "Oh crap! I can't lie to my mom. Alright, I confess." She shuffled to a chair beside her mother, pulling Amos along, still grasping her handcuffs. The wooden chair spokes creaked as she sat down heavily. "When you hear the whole story, you'll agree it wasn't my fault. I couldn't help myself."

All other conversation in the room stopped. Officer Smith, Farlow, and I leaned closer. The crowd of strangers edged forward. The room was silent while we waited to hear her story.

Rosemary cleared her throat. "It began about a month ago. One day Sage was bored and sneaked into our father's computer." She landed a kick on her brother's ankle. "He was always doing that, pretending to be a computer hacker."

Rosemary raised her eyes to glare at Clair, who was peeking out from behind Gloria. "This time Sage found something. A whole file devoted to that hussy. There was all sort of information about her and about this town." The young woman shook her head and snarled. "But the worst part was the photos."

Gasps erupted from the group of strangers.

I glanced at Clair, trying to imagine what kind of photos Giles might have. She popped out from behind Gloria and waved her hands. "No way. He never took photos of me, and I've never in my life posed for revealing pictures." She faced Rosemary. "Those were my photos your father stole from my web page." Whirling around to the audience of strangers, Clair declared her innocence. "They're all modest and proper."

Rosemary shrugged and directed a response to the onlookers. "What's it matter what kind they were? They were pictures of her."

She turned her attention to her mother. "After Sage found that file, we kept an eye on father. And one weekend he traveled out of town, but he wasn't where he said he would be. So we traced him to Evelynton. We figured he'd planned a secret liaison with his girlfriend."

My curiosity got the best of me. "How did you locate him? He wasn't using his own name. I checked. I had to drive around and show a picture." I shot a glance at Farlow hoping he hadn't noticed me confess to snooping. Fortunately, his attention focused on Rosemary.

She continued. "He always used the name Bob Smith when traveling incognito, so I called a few places until I found him. It was easy. Not many spots to hide in this town."

Sage took up the story. "There was only one thing we could do. We got in the car and drove here. He was surprised to see us when we showed up at his room that night. Of course he played innocent and denied everything, but we had the proof. Why would he have those photos if she wasn't his girlfriend?"

Ophelia put both hands over her face. "I can't believe it."

Her son glanced at her and continued. "Finally, he confessed his infatuation with the real estate woman. He even said he planned to convince her to go away with him."

Sage gave up fanning his mother and took a chair beside Rosemary. "I guess the Lane woman had turned him down. But he insisted he'd never give up, since she was the only woman he could love."

At that point, there was a loud sob from Ophelia, and Rosemary put her arm around her. "Sorry Mom."

Ophelia patted Rosemary's hand. "It's okay, dear. I suppose it was mid-life crisis."

Rosemary resumed scowling at Clair. "We tried to convince him to come home, but he said he'd found his dream girl. You can imagine, about that time I was getting really mad."

Rosemary twisted to face her mother. "I couldn't stand it any longer. Tried to control my temper like you taught me. I even went to the mini-fridge to get some water to cool down. And there it was."

Officer Farlow flipped a page in his notebook and leaned in. "There what was?"

"A roll of cookie dough—frozen solid. Father never noticed it in my hand. He kept on ranting about that skinny hussy."

Rosemary stared at the far wall as she recounted the assault. "I went crazy and clobbered him with the dough. Once I got into the swing of things, I kept it up until he fell down. But he got up again and crawled on to the bed."

She lifted a shoulder. "I couldn't believe he was still declaring his love for Clair Lane, so I hit him a few more times. Then he shut up."

Sage gripped the arms of the chair. "You see, officer, it was obvious I couldn't help him. It was too late. He quit moving and we both knew he was dead. That pretty much shocked my sister into her right mind."

Rosemary nodded. "It did."

Sage continued. "We sat in the room for a while and discussed the pros and cons of calling the police. In the end, we decided we should dispose of his body. We wouldn't want mother to see him in the condition he was in. So we wrapped him up in the blanket, carried him out, and put him in the trunk of his rental car. I drove it and Sis followed."

Farlow scribbled in his notebook. "So, he's in the car. Then what?"

Rosemary shrugged. "I'd told Sage to find a dumpster that was easy to get to, but to make sure it wasn't out in the open. When he found one, we had a terrible time getting father's body out of the trunk." She slowly shook her head. "Talk about dead weight."

Sage rolled his eyes and nodded.

Rosemary continued. "Finally, we did and managed to put it in the dumpster. We found a spot to leave our father's car, and went back to clean up the room. Packed up all his things and drove back home that same night."

Having finished her statement, Rosemary relaxed into her chair. "Man, it's been a long day. Do you have an espresso?"

Chapter Twenty-One

My to-do list was empty. I could find nothing to worry about. The sun warmed my face and the birds sang. I walked into town, leaving the Chrysler at home. My only goal for the day was to stop at Ava's for a quick cup of her new coffee drink, the Tranquil Toddy. I loved the name. It filled me with pleasant expectations.

Reaching for the Java's front door, I recognized Anita peering out at me through the glass. She pushed it open, juggling two carry out cups and small white paper bag. With a little shriek, my friend indicated that we should step to the side to chat.

Anita steadied a cup with her chin. "Hey, girlfriend. What have you been doing these last few days? I've been trying to catch up on cleaning at home. Working at the Java during the festival wore me out."

"The same for me. Except I didn't work during the festival and I haven't been cleaning my house." I shrugged. "But the craziness in the food alley was more stress than I needed. And then going with Clair to the police station. Don't get me wrong, catching the killer was exhilarating. But I'm ready for peace and relaxation."

Anita resettled the items she carried. "I'm disappointed I missed the fun. Really wish I'd been there to hear the confession. I could have written 'Case closed by the Women's Detective Agency.' in my notebook. We can still use it for publicity, when we decide to take on another case."

"No! I'm getting too old for crime fighting and I think I can say the same for Clair. She's been holed up in her house for the last three days, resting. And you know she never stays home."

Anita blew out a breath. "You girls are just acting old. We're only in our forties. Anyway, I'm glad I ran into you. We should make a date for coffee, soon."

"Gosh. We haven't talked for a while. You know, I never even heard who won the Marshmallow Festival Cook-off. I guessed it wasn't Ava, since there's no sign in the window. Was it Carl from Burgers 'N Bean Sprouts? Please tell me he didn't."

Anita shook her head. "Nope. It wasn't Carl, and I heard he was fit to be tied. He'd been counting on his buddy, the mayor, to give him the prize."

"I shouldn't be thinking negative thoughts about him. Rarity would shake her finger at me. I'm sure he's a nice guy, but I don't ever want to see the Vegi-Mallow." My mouth puckered thinking about it. "So, who won?"

"Funniest thing. It was Marci Johnson." At my quizzical look, she continued. "She has that little cake shop on Short Street. She entered a custom made smores and created everything from scratch— marshmallow, graham cracker, and chocolate bar. We'll have to go over there some time and try one."

Anita edged toward the street. "Right now, I gotta run. I promised Jake I'd bring him coffee and Killer Marshmallow Fudge Brownies, so I better get them home while they're still warm. He's so looking forward to it."

Anita crossed to the parking lot, and I went into the Java. The place was quiet, just what I was looking for. I picked up the Toddy and claimed my table.

The Tranquil Toddy was hot, smooth, chocolaty, and amazingly soothing. I closed my eyes and savored each sip, slipping into my private little imaginary world. I didn't hear the footsteps of a visitor approach the table, and only glanced up when the chair beside me slid out.

"Do you mind if I sit for a minute?" Not waiting for an answer, Officer Farlow sat.

The Tranquil Toddy must have been true to its name. I remained calm and managed to utter a greeting.

I watched Farlow settle into the seat and acknowledged the coffee mug in his hand. "Officer Farlow, I didn't know you were a fan of Ava's Java. Do you come here often?" The only time I'd seen him in the coffee shop was the day Giles Gold turned up in the dumpster. Not my favorite memory.

"Please, call me Jim. I'm not on a case."

What? Who was this man?

Farlow took a sip of his coffee. "No. Usually I think one brand is as good as another, so I take mine at the station. But Amos says drinking Ava's Java will change my mind."

He tipped up the mug again. "He's right. It's pretty good."

We sat for an awkward moment, both sipping our coffee and avoiding eye contact.

Farlow cleared his throat. "Lauren, I want you to know I appreciate your help with the Giles Gold case."

There he was, using my first name again. I'd come to the conclusion that the wild day at the station had been real, not a dream, but this meeting had me wondering again.

Farlow was still talking. "You do tend to interfere and get in the way of official police work. But I believe you have good intentions. And I admit your instincts are sound. A sharp eye for detail. You probably missed your calling. Should have been in law enforcement."

I stared at him for a moment. I hadn't noticed how blue his eyes were. Or that he had a cute dimple on one side of his mouth.

He was waiting. I needed to respond on the chance this was not a dream. "Thank you, Officer Farlow. I mean...Jim." That felt weird and I never wanted to say it again. "That's very kind of you. But the truth is I don't have good instincts when it comes to criminals. I'm almost always wrong in my first guess. I have stumbled across the real criminal a time or two. But by accident, not by design."

Farlow shook his head. "On the contrary, take Gladys's testimony about the dumpster. I would have passed her off as a crazy old lady. But you pushed in and questioned Rosemary and Sage Gold, yourself. Good job."

I felt a blush creeping in, and mumbled. "Thank you."

I tipped my cup and watched the Tranquil Toddy swirl around. "Since we're on the subject. There's something I've been wondering. Do you believe Rosemary Gold's explanation for her violent outbursts? Isn't caffeine over-load a bit farfetched?"

Officer Farlow chuckled and shook his head. "That was a new one on me. Didn't believe it for a second. But I looked it up. Turns out that same defense has been used by others in at least two cases, back in 2009. I think they called it psychosis due to caffeine overdose, or something like that. It looks as if she might get away with it."

"Huh. It's hard for me to believe anyone could overdose on caffeine. At least you solved the case. What the judge decides is his business."

We sat quietly and awkwardly for another moment. Finally, Officer Farlow placed his cup on the table and eyed me. "I have to tell you I'm disturbed about one thing. We still have a loose end. The murder weapon. What happened to it? Chief Stoddard will be back to work next week, and I'd really like to get that pinned down. The Golds have clammed up. They were real talkative about everything else but won't say a word about the weapon."

Farlow leaned toward me. "What are your thoughts? Is there a chance of finding it?"

The man was asking my opinion. My hand trembled, and I wracked my brain for something to say. What if he never asked again? If only I could think of something intelligent.

I took a breath and began spitting out ideas as they popped into my head. "They could have thrown it into another garbage can. Or maybe they tossed it in Beaver Creek, although they would have had to drive blocks out of their way to get there. Oh crap, if it's been in the water it wouldn't be intact. Unless of course it was really well wrapped. So that's still a possibility."

I took time to breathe. "How about their homes in New York? Has anyone searched there?"

Officer Farlow pulled out his notebook. "Those are good thoughts. I'm afraid that if they used another garbage can, it would be in the dump by now." He pointed his pen at me. "I'll send someone out there to take a look." He made a note. "We don't have the equipment to search the creek." He shook his head. "Never had the need before."

He smacked the notebook on the table. "Wait. I think there's a scuba club that meets at the Y." He made another note and finished with, "I'll call New York authorities and have them send a team to search their homes."

Farlow sat back and picked up his coffee again. "These are long shots, and we don't have much time to check them out."

Things were going so well, I wanted to be encouraging. "But remember, even if you don't find it, you have the confession. Chief Stoddard will be impressed with that"

Farlow blew out a breath. "Maybe, but I hate to leave the case unfinished. It's discouraging. There will always be a big question mark in the file. A missing murder weapon."

I heard the heavy footsteps behind me and a cheerful whoop. "Hey, Jimmy. Didn't know you were in here." Officer Amos Smith ambled up to the table. "Hi, Ms. Halloren. How's everything? Mind if I join you?"

Amos sank into the third chair at the table. "Isn't it

great to have the town quiet again? The Festival is over and the business owners are happy. It was a big success. Best of all, the murder was solved. Life is good."

It was a good thing Amos was smiling. I'd begun to worry that if my friends happened to notice me through the window, sitting with these two, they'd be out collecting bail money.

Officer Smith scratched his head. "I'm glad it's over. But I have to admit I was surprised that Rosemary Gold did it. She was always cooperative, and seemed really nice."

Smith chuckled and glanced at Farlow. "Remember she even brought in snacks for everyone in the office. We were all surprised she would do that, particularly when her mother was unhappy with our investigation. You commented about how someone was finally showing appreciation for the work we do. I don't remember anyone ever bringing us cookies. Do you, Jimmy?"

Officer Farlow shook his head. "I think she's the only person ever to show real appreciation for our efforts. At least, in my years of service."

Amos hummed and a big smile crossed his face. "Those were good cookies. I wouldn't mind having more of them. Do you suppose, now that she's in jail, Miss. Gold would give me the recipe? I told my wife about how tasty they were, and I know she'd like to try her hand at a batch."

Farlow shrugged. "You can ask. Now that she's cooled her heals in a cell for a while, she might give it to you."

Amos glanced at his watch. "Guess I better get back to the station, since you're in here. Can't have both of us taking a break."

He gave Farlow and me a nod and pushed up from the table. "I think I'll see if Ava has any of those Killer Marshmallow Brownies left."

My brain was spinning. My foot was tapping. I clamped my mouth shut for fear of getting into trouble again. I bit my tongue, and had to hold myself in my chair. It was time to use those deep breathing exercises.

This was the first time Jimmy Farlow had been nice to me, ever. If I blurted out my suspicion, would it spoil the moment? I slanted my gaze at him and waited.

Farlow took another sip of coffee and stopped with his cup in the air. "All that time Amos thought Rosemary was showing us her gratitude, but she probably figured she could sweeten our opinion of her. All criminals think they're smarter than the police. You heard Amos. She nearly fooled him. I suppose for a while I was taken in, too. But I know even people who seem nice commit murder."

He chuckled. "Yep. Those were good cookies, though. Good…"

Farlow's coffee mug clunked to the table and his hand went to his forehead. "No. It can't be." Through clenched teeth, he said, "It can't be!"

I raised an eyebrow, but fought hard not to smile.

He ran a hand through his hair and mumbled, "The cookies."

Those blue eyes locked with mine. I pressed my lips together and gave a slow nod.

Farlow closed his eyes. "We ate the murder weapon!"

The End

CAFFEINATED MURDER

Would you like to Help the Author?

Do you love the quirky characters of Evelynton, Indiana? Help others find my books.

Tell your friends about my novels.

Read my books where others can see.

Leave a review on Amazon.com and goodreads.com. It doesn't have to be long. Even a short note is an encouragement and makes it possible for me to keep writing.

Comment on my Facebook Author page or my Blog.

Born and raised in Northeastern Indiana, Lynne Waite
Chapman is a lover of mystery and suspense. In September
of 2016, she published her first cozy mystery. The debut
novel Heart Strings—first in the Evelynton Murder series—
was a 2016 semi-finalist in the American Christian Fiction
Writers Association Genesis contest. The next three in the
series, Heart Beat, Murderous Heart, and Caffeinated
Murder continue the adventures of three friends in the small
town Evelynton, Indiana.
Lynne Waite Chapman began her writing career with fifteen
years of composing weekly non-fiction content for the
BellaOnline.com Hair site, drawing on her thirty plus years
as a hairdresser. Retiring the Hair site, she has spent the last
fifteen years sharing her faith and penning weekly content
for the BellaOnline.com Christian Living site.
She is a regular contributor of devotions for several print
publications and devotionals, and has written articles for
many church bulletins and newsletters. She has also
contributed articles to numerous internet publications.

For more information about current and past writing projects
visit Lynne at:
https://www.lynnechapman.com

Find her on Facebook at:
https://www.facebook.com/LynneWaiteChapmanAuthor

Follow her Amazon Author page:
http://www.amazon.com/author/lwchapman

GoodReads:

https://www.goodreads.com/LynneWaiteChapman

Follow her on Twitter:
@LWChapmanAuthor

Instagram:
https://www.instagram.com/lynnewaite/

Made in the USA
Monee, IL
28 September 2020

43475644R00100